BOYFRIEND GLASSES

Livia Harper

BOYFRIEND
GLASSES
A NOVEL
LIVIA
HARPER

This is a work of fiction. Names, characters, places, and incidents either are the product of the author's imagination, or are used fictitiously. Any resemblance to actual persons, living or dead, events, or locales, are entirely coincidental.

ISBN: 1517375312
ISBN-13: 978-1517375317

For Dave, who is thankfully nothing like anyone in this book.

Part One

My Blake

1

SOME PEOPLE SAY THERE'S NO such thing as love at first sight. They're wrong.

The first time I saw Blake … well, it was like his heart was a magnet and mine was molten nickel. I could feel the fire of it singe my skin as it left my body. I could see its hot cord twining orange out of my chest, melting its way directly toward his. When our hearts met, they fused. Mine wrapped around his, holding him forever.

I knew it was love because the first time I saw him, the very first time, Blake did something no one else had ever done before. Blake made me forget all about Johnny.

We were at a geeks/Greeks party at the Sigma Phi Upsilon house before I knew to call it SigUp. It was the first real party of many that night, the first party night of the year. We were drunk on freedom and electric with high expectations for our future. Walking in there with Amber like we belonged, like it was no big deal, like they threw parties just so girls like us would come? It made me feel wild and alive for the first time since Johnny. It was everything I hoped college would be. It was everything high school wasn't.

Blake was … all Blake. There's no other way to say it. There's no other way to define all the little parts that add up to him being him—his confident smile, his body tall and statuesque, the absolute command he had of the whole room. Dark hair and tan skin and eyes like peridot: green and shimmering and endless. He was all Blake.

Every single girl in the room was looking at him. Every single one. Why wouldn't they? He was perfect.

But Blake didn't pay attention to any of them. He knew what he wanted, and he knew he would get it. And what he wanted was me. Right from the beginning. He could feel me there, in that room, feel our connection just like I could.

But he saw Amber first. And he got confused.

He walked right up to her like I wasn't even there. He didn't say a word, just held her eyes and took her hand and led her into a corner. Everyone stared as he took his fake black glasses off and put them on her and kissed her. They looked like the perfect couple. But we would have been better, so much better.

Amber wore those glasses all night, a trophy of his love. Her cornsilk eyelashes brushed against them, every flutter reminding her she was his choice. His.

I wanted to rip those glasses off her face, just to touch something he'd touched.

But I don't want to anymore. I don't have to. I'm wearing

them right now.

And Amber is dead.

Part Two

My Amber

2

I'VE SPENT THE LAST THREE months working out and studying every fashion magazine I can get my hands on. My desk back home is stacked high with issues of *In Style*, *Vogue*, *Marie Claire*, everything—even teen ones like *Seventeen* and *Ms.*, each of them highlighted and dog-eared like a textbook. Between stocking shelves in my dad's gas station and sliding change through bulletproof glass, I scoured them for beauty tips. Then I took every penny of my earnings to buy blush and shoes and haircuts from the best salons all the way in the city.

I have been plucked and dyed and polished until *I am* those glossy images. My tangle of red hair has been tamed into smooth curls that bounce down my back. My eyebrows are perfectly tweezed, and my lips perfectly plumped. I am a butterfly emerged from her cocoon. I am I am I am. You wouldn't even recognize me now.

But Johnny will. I can't wait for him to.

It's all for him, of course. For Johnny. I thought maybe if

I looked more like those girls in the magazines, more like *that girl*, Johnny would see me as I really am. He would see all I was meant to be and know, just like I do, that we're perfect for each other. With every new shade of lipstick and every new summer dress, I'd stare out of my glass cage in the gas station, looking toward the parking lot, hoping to see his beat up white Impala drive in.

He never came.

Then I found out his family moved, and no one would tell me where.

I still look for him, but now it's on my drives into the city, in the streets and grocery stores and coffee shops of the towns that line the highway. How far could they have gone? Maybe far. It hurts to think about.

Everyone says it's time to put Johnny aside, but they don't know about true love. I believe, deep in my heart, that we're meant to be together. And people who are meant to be together will find each other eventually.

In the meantime, I have to become his perfect match. I have to go to college and be successful and have the kinds of friends that will let him know there is only one path.

His destiny.

Me.

I look for Johnny constantly on this drive, this big, important drive all the way from my tiny town in the rural Colorado plains. It marks the beginning of a whole new life for me. College! A fresh start!

But it also takes me so far away from where we met that it makes me nervous. I'll be in the southeast corner of Pennsylvania. What if he comes back for me? What would my parents tell him?

Probably nothing. They never liked Johnny.

I stop at a gas station even though I don't need gas. It's part of my routine now. Johnny could be there. You never know.

This gas station is the last one before I get there. I take my time filling up, count until twenty cars have passed in and out of the lot before going inside. It keeps me here longer, gives me a better chance of seeing him.

Inside, I wander every aisle, picking up and putting down all kinds of stuff before deciding on nothing. I'm not even really looking at the items. I'm scanning the aisles, watching the door every time I hear it ding. But I don't see his face.

At the restrooms, I pretend to go through the wrong door by mistake, then stand there fake-frozen, scanning the men's room for his back, his hands, his face. An annoyed businessman turns his hips away from me fast, spraying the already filthy wall. A huge trucker catches my eye and chuckles. I turn and go. Johnny isn't in there.

To sell the lie, I go into the women's room even though I don't need to go and sit in the stall for a few more minutes than anyone needs to. Then I change into my dress.

By the time I leave, none of the men are still lingering in the store. I take one last look around just to be sure Johnny hasn't come in while I've been inside, then drive away.

I try to tell myself it doesn't matter. When we're supposed to find each other, we will.

3

THE GRAY BLOCK BUILDING LOOMS large against a bright blue sky dotted with tall oaks just now kissed with auburn. The building is twenty stories high and looks like it was built in the sixties. The sign below the flat awning reads: Candel Hall. My dorm. I park in one of the last available spots, far away from the entrance.

There are students everywhere, hauling tubs of clothes and bright new bedding, posters of their favorite bands rolled into tight tubes over their shoulders. One boy has brown hair, cut looser and freer just like Johnny's, but it's not him. He's not even close to as beautiful as Johnny.

My Johnny, my Johnny, my beautiful boy. No one will ever be like you.

A pretty blond girl walks ahead of a rolling cart, which is being pushed by her dad. It's packed with teal-colored everything: a teal lamp with a teal toile shade, a teal chair covered in teal fur, a teal flowered rug, a whiteboard with a teal border, and a teal shower tote with a teal loofah swinging from the handle.

I'm suddenly worried. I've only been thinking about what *I* looked like, not what *my room* is supposed to look like. The baby pink chintz quilt my grandmother sewed by hand, the one that's been sitting dutifully on my bed since I was four, suddenly seems shabby by comparison. How did I not think of this?

My throat gets tight, and I have to suck in a heap of air to calm down. I have to do something. I have to do something. I have to—

I can fix this.

There's a mall five miles away. I'll run over and buy all new things and ditch my old, ratty trunk in a dumpster.

How much is that going to cost? I perform a quick tally of the cash in my wallet: I don't have enough. I've spent nearly every penny just to get here and will need to get a part-time job as soon as I can if I want to do anything but go to classes and eat in the cafeteria.

There's the money my dad gave me for textbooks, five new one hundred dollar bills my mom told me would be the last money I'd ever see from them. But classes start Monday. There's no way I can get a job before Monday. So what's worse? Making a bad first impression? Or struggling through classes without books for a couple weeks?

I can catch up. I've always been a good student. I can talk to my professors or read the books in the bookstore or try to borrow them from other students.

What I can't do is let people see my old, awful things. If

they saw that quilt, they'd know right away. They'd only see that other girl, the one I used to be. The ugly, awkward, high-school nothing. They wouldn't see the person I am now, the one I've worked so hard to become.

Screw the books.

My key is in the ignition, the rabbit's foot dangling and ready, when there's a tapping on my window.

"Greta?" My aunt's face stares down at me, round and grinning and surrounded by springy brown curls. No, no, no, no, no. This can't be happening. Not now. I roll down the window.

"Hey, chicky-poo! You excited? How was your drive?"

"Good," I say with a forced smile. "I didn't know you'd be here." I had thought, in fact, I'd be able to avoid Aunt Peggy for at least a few weeks.

I didn't want to go to Culford University. It's not a bad school. In fact, it's a prestigious school—top-tier and second only to the Ivy Leagues. But it has no real film program and is, therefore, the last place Johnny will go. But my parents refused to pay for college at all, so my options were limited. When Aunt Peggy volunteered to cover my costs, going to Culford (her alma mater) was her only condition.

She only lives a couple miles away from campus, so I had to put up a fight to live in the dorms. She wanted me to stay with her so she could keep an eye on me. It was my insistence that dorm life was a quintessential part of the college experience that finally convinced her—not my good grades in high school or all my efforts to prove I could handle myself after what happened with Johnny. I told her living in the dorms was something I needed to get a fresh start. And wasn't that the whole point of going to college at all? Besides, I'd told her, she'd still be nearby. She'd still be there just in case I needed her. What a joke. I knew I wouldn't.

"I wanted to surprise you! Your mom told me you were arriving today." Of course she did. Aunt Peggy is playing this off as nothing, but it was probably a plan hatched up by her and my mom. Mom, still trying to interfere even though she practically shoved me out the door. "Did you hit some traffic on the highway? I thought you'd be here sooner."

"Yes, traffic," I say, trying to paste a smile on my face. "An accident on I-70 just before Topeka. Shut down both lanes. I was stuck overnight." There was no accident, of course, just my searching. Aunt Peggy can't know about the searching.

"I hope no one was hurt."

"I don't know. The ambulances were gone by the time I got there." An awkward moment passes. She seems to be waiting for me to do something, but I can't tell what.

"Ready to check out your new digs?"

"Actually, I just realized I need to run to the store for a few things. It was so nice for you to come out to see me, though. Can I meet you for dinner sometime this week?"

"The store? There're only a few minutes left before they close the check-in desk for the day, honey. You've got to get in there, or you're gonna get stuck bunking with me for the night." She laughs, even though she knows I fought against living with her.

I glance at the clock. Shit. She's right.

"Of course. I lost track of the time." Reluctantly, I get out of the car. "Sorry. It's been a long day."

"You must be tired, all that driving. What'd it take you? Two days? Three?"

"Three." I turn to walk toward the building. She motions toward the lone trunk in my back seat, an old thing that used to belong to my grandmother, left to rot in the basement for decades.

"Don't you want to take a load in on our way?" she says.

"That's okay. I'd rather see the room first. I might not bring everything in."

"What do you mean? You brought it all this way. What else would you do with it?"

"I didn't mean—I meant right away. I just want to make sure there's room for everything in the elevator."

"It doesn't look like you brought much. I'm sure it'll fit."

"I don't want to take it up right now, okay?" I say, unable to hide the edge in my voice. She stares at me, searching my face for something. The other girl. The old me.

I force myself to soften my face. To smile. "Sorry. I'm just really tired. And really excited to see my room. Would you mind if we go up first?"

"Okay, honey, sure," she says. We walk toward the door. "You know, I'm really glad you picked Culford. It'll give us a chance to get to know each other better."

"Me too," I say as she puts her arm around me. "Me too."

As if it was a choice.

4

FLOOR-TO-CEILING MIRRORS PANEL the elevator. I check myself while the floors tick their way up to seventeen. My lipstick is still perfect. I smooth down the flyaways in my curls. And then I notice the wrinkles in my dress.

It should be flawless. I only changed ten minutes ago in the restroom of the gas station for precisely this reason. But the short drive has ironed creases under my rear and at my middle, pointing out exactly where the material stretches to accommodate my flaws. I've slimmed down a lot since graduation, but I still have some weight to lose, and now the dress screams it. I pull on the fabric to smooth it down, but it sets back into unflattering lines as soon as I release it.

"You look great," Aunt Peggy says.

"No, I don't," I say.

"Relax. She's going to love you."

But what if she doesn't?

The elevator dings and we're here. There's a clang of activity in the narrow corridor. Students and their parents carry boxes and hangers full of clothes down the halls. People seem to stream continuously in and out of rooms with no apparent pattern. An acne-pocked blond boy races past, another guy shouting at his heels, and his shoulder knocks mine as he passes.

"Sorry," he shouts without even looking back at me. Will I be invisible here too? Maybe everyone was right. Maybe I'm not ready for this.

"Come on," my Aunt says. It's only then I realize I'm standing still. She tugs my hand, and I follow her toward room 1717. The door is ajar. Aunt Peggy taps on it and enters.

"Hello?" she calls. I yank my hand away from hers just in time.

There's a girl standing on one of the two beds, hanging a corkboard loaded with pictures of her friends. Pretty friends. Happy friends. Pink sweat-pantsed friends and cheerleader friends and friends in lavish prom dresses. I have no photos. None. There was nothing to take photos of.

Two older women, one who looks like her mom and one who looks like her grandmother, unpack clothes into a wardrobe standing against a wall. They all turn to look at us.

"You must be Greta!" the girl says and hops off the bed. Her name is Amber, which I only know from my dorm assignment letter. She is blond and southern and perfect, and I am terrified. I had hoped she was pretty, had hoped I wouldn't get stuck with someone who would make things hard, but I didn't expect her to be this pretty. She must think I'm disgusting with my wrinkled dress and my frizzy red hair and my cheap purse. I don't even know what to say.

But before I can think of anything or even nod my head that yes, I am Greta, she throws her arms around me and hugs me tight. She's stronger than she looks.

"Sorry. I'm a hugger," she says in a sweet twang. "You're gonna have to get used to that 'cause I can't seem to stop myself. I love a good hug. I also love Ryan Gosling and coconut *anything* and all animals. Except cats. I'm deathly allergic. It's the tragedy of my life." She finally lets me go. "And my name's Amber, but you probably put that together already." She motions to the beds, "I hope you don't mind, but I took the one on the left. They looked pretty much the same, so I figured it wouldn't be a big deal either way. But if you'd rather have it I can totally move my stuff over to the other side. It's no big deal at all. I also thought we might get a little more space in here if we bunked them. I saw some other girls do that down the hall. Do you like top or bottom?"

I am dazzled by the aqua clarity of her eyes and couldn't force my mouth to open even if I knew the right words to say.

"Give the girl a chance to catch her breath, darlin'," the one who's probably Amber's mom says, "You're scaring the poor thing to death." She steps forward in her pressed linen pants (no wrinkles—how?!), grinning wide underneath a perfect blond bob. "I'm Evelyn, Amber's momma. It's a pleasure to meet you."

"Don't say 'momma,' Momma. It makes me sound like an infant."

"I am her momma, whether she likes it or not, and this is *my* momma, Bunny." Amber's grandmother steps forward, as perfectly manicured and made up as her daughter and granddaughter, her short hair set in an elegant silver wave against her cheek.

"Nice to meet you," I say. "All of you."

"It is a pleasure to meet you, sweetheart," Bunny says, clutching my hand in both of hers. She hooks her elbow around mine and leans in conspiratorially. "Don't worry. Amber's not as bad as she seems at first. She can actually be quite pleasant when she makes an effort. *If* she makes an effort, that is."

"Granny!" Amber shouts with a grin. "Don't be puttin' ideas into her head."

I let out a nervous laugh.

Aunt Peggy steps forward, beaming, to shake Evelyn's hand. "I'm Peggy."

I'm suddenly glad Aunt Peggy is here. Everyone seems to have parents around today. It might look weird if I didn't have anyone.

"Well, don't you have just the prettiest little girl," Evelyn says to Aunt Peggy. "That red hair! Stunning!" She thinks I'm stunning?

"Oh, I'm her aunt. Peggy Danforth. Her mother is my sister."

"How nice of you to bring her to school like this."

"She drove herself. All the way from Colorado on her own if you can believe it. I live here in Pennsylvania. Right in Culford, actually."

Evelyn turns to me, "Aren't you lucky, having family so close?"

Something like that. I nod yes and smile.

"We're just torn apart having Amber so far away. We're from all the way in Georgia. But she had her heart set. I suppose that's the nature of things." Evelyn sighs then smiles to Aunt Peggy. "You know, it makes me feel a whole lot better that the girls will have an adult nearby. It really does."

"I'm just around the corner if they need anything," Aunt Peggy says. "They can come by anytime."

Fantastic.

"Well isn't that just sweet of you. Thank you."

An older man enters, big as a football player, sandy-haired and tan, wearing khaki shorts and a pink polo shirt, the kind with a little alligator on it. "Hunted up a screwdriver. Let me have at that bookshelf."

"Daddy, this is Greta, my roommate."

"Greta! Of the Garbo Greta's?"

I don't understand what he means. The confusion must register on my face.

"Just kidding. I'm Paul. Pleased to meet you, kid." He winks at me and throws an arm around his daughter. "You two aren't planning on getting into any trouble now, are you?"

"They better not," Bunny says with a raised eyebrow.

"Why else do you go to college?" he says.

"Don't you start," Evelyn says. Then she turns to me. "Now, Greta, you're just going to have to sit down and tell us every little thing about yourself."

5

THE REST OF THE DAY goes by in a blur. Paul helps Aunt Peggy and I unpack my car. Miraculously, they coo over my bedspread instead of thinking it's frumpy. It must be the way I look now. I've noticed this about people: the better you look, the better everyone thinks you are as a whole person. They're willing to give you a pass on things that would otherwise get you made fun of.

We go out to dinner with all of Amber's family. Aunt Peggy picks the place because she knows the town. It's a custom salad place that's delicious and across the street from campus, but probably too expensive to eat at very often. Aunt Peggy is a health nut, and the choice worries me for a moment—what if they're meat and potatoes people? But everyone compliments her choice. Paul fights with Aunt Peggy over the check and wins. Aunt Peggy goes straight home from the restaurant, and Amber's family drops us back at the dorm and goes to their hotel. They've invited me to breakfast tomorrow morning, which will be the last time they see Amber before flying home.

I snuggle under the quilt as Amber comes out of the bathroom. We have our very own bathroom. Well, sort of. It connects our room with the one next door, which is home to a couple of shy girls named Katie and Sally. The bathroom is just a sink and a toilet, no shower, but it's nice to not have to walk down the hall in the middle of the night. Amber gets into bed and turns off her light.

"What a day," she says.

"I know," I say.

"Wanna place bets on who cries most tomorrow? You're probably gonna say my momma, but I'd put money on Daddy."

"Really?"

"Oh yeah, he's a gusher."

"You'd never know it."

"Just wait. You'll see," she says. "So now that the parents are gone, I want to know the juicy stuff. Got any boyfriends back home?"

"Sort of," I say. "I don't know. Not really, I guess."

"It's complicated, right?"

"Very."

"I know what you mean. I've been dating this boy Andrew since homecoming junior year. He wanted to keep it up even though he's going all the way out to Stanford. He's really smart. But, I don't know. Momma says we're both gonna change so much."

"Exactly," I say. "I'm going to be an entirely different

person the next time I see him. I already am."

"It's hard to believe, isn't it? We're here. College. Everything's going to be different now."

"Everything."

"So what's his name, you're guy? I want to know the whole story." This is nice. Already, Amber feels like a sister. Like more than a sister. It seems like I can tell her anything.

"Johnny," I say. "And he's perfect. There's no way I'm going to meet anyone like him ever again."

"What's he like?"

"Tall. Golden brown hair. Sweet. He's going to be a movie director someday."

"Really?"

"Yeah. He's so talented. You should see the films he makes. They're amazing."

"Where's he going to school?"

Shit. I don't know. I've called every film school in the country, but none of them would tell me if he was enrolled or not.

"Um, he's taking a year off to travel around Europe. He wants to get a little life experience before starting college." It could be true.

"And you didn't want to go with him?"

Oh no. Now I look like an idiot. "He didn't … my parents didn't think it was a good idea."

"Did he break your heart? Boys can do that, can't they?"

"No! He would never do that. Not intentionally, at least. The time away will be good for us. It's like you said, we're both about to change so much." I tug the blankets up to my chin. "But I know, in my heart, he's the one."

"That's so romantic. I didn't feel the same about Andrew, I guess. I liked him, sure. But I think I stayed with him so long because all his friends were my friends and all my friends were his friends, you know? I don't think I ever really felt that *thing*. Or maybe I did but I wasn't paying attention. I do get distracted from time to time."

"You would know. When you feel it—I don't know—it's like your whole heart rips out of your chest. There's no way to describe it. I felt it right away with Johnny. The moment I met him."

"Really? How'd you meet?"

"At school, junior year. We didn't have any classes together, so I didn't even notice him until we bumped into each other in the lunchroom. He spilled orange juice all over my favorite white button-down."

"You're kidding me!"

"No. It was totally ruined of course. But he was a complete gentleman about it. He gave me his sweater to cover it up, and then he had to go around wearing only a T-shirt the whole rest of the day. And it was really cold. He must have been freezing."

"How valiant."

"I still have that sweater."

Everything I tell Amber about Johnny is true. Well, mostly everything. We did meet when he spilled his juice all over me in the lunch line. He did give me his sweater. Only later, when he asked for it back, I told him I had lost it.

I never lost it. I would never be so careless with anything he gave me.

Amber sighs. "That's the kind of story you can tell your grandkids someday. It really is. I want a story like that. Andrew's a friend of the family. I've known him since we were babies. It's so boring I could cry." Amber yawns until her face is nearly all mouth. "Well, I'm glad you've got a little romance in your life. I'll just have to live vicariously through you for a while."

"You'll meet someone. I know you will. Everyone says it usually happens in college."

"Honestly, I'm not totally sure I even want to right now," she says. "I mean, aren't you just a little bit excited about all these boys? I saw at least four guys on our floor who looked so scrumptious I could eat them right up."

She laughs, and I join in, even though I don't think it's very funny.

"I feel like I want to taste everything right now, you know? Not order the same thing every day. Takeout! That's my plan. For a while at least."

This, I don't really understand, so I don't say anything. I let the silence fall between us, between the glow of the streetlights that haze up into our window and the low thump of someone's music in a floor far, far below. Isn't love—one true, special love—more valuable than a hundred kisses from strangers? It is to me.

"Anyway, it's getting late," she says, "and Lord knows

they'll show up bright and early tomorrow. We better get some sleep."

"Yeah, you're right."

"'Night roomie," she says, and I can hear the smile in her words.

"'Night roomie," I say.

I have a friend.

Part Three

My Johnny

6

AFTER I MEET JOHNNY, I sign up to be his friend on Facebook. It's easy. He's the kind of guy who likes everybody back and has lots of friends. At first, I only check his posts at night before I go to bed. Then I just go to the computer lab at lunch to see real quick if there's anything new. But after a while, I sneak to my phone between every class just so I can see if he's posted anything.

We aren't allowed to have phones in class; they discourage us from bringing them to school at all. Of course, everybody does it. Most people keep them close all day, but my parents have a strict policy that if I'm caught with a phone in class they'll take it away until I graduate. They're not the kind of people who make idle threats. It was too much of a risk, until Johnny. Now it's worth it.

Usually, there's nothing new on his page. You have to be really sneaky to pull off posting on Facebook during class, and Johnny isn't really the sneaky type. He's very honest and very trustworthy. But every now and then there's something there. Maybe a video of somebody doing something crazy on a skateboard, or a link to some movie he's amped up about, or a picture of him and his friends eating lunch outside. The lunch ones sometimes hurt to see, but then I remember boys get really nervous about asking girls out. That must be why he hasn't asked me out yet. I try not to let it bother me.

All my watching pays off the very first week. On Facebook that Thursday afternoon is this:

Midnight premier of THE Z-FORCE III tonight. Be there or suffer the wrath of Zelon!

Johnny loves movies. They're his favorite thing in the world. He's in the filmmaking club at school and makes these amazing movies with his friends. One day he'll probably ask me to star in one.

And this post? It has to be an invitation, a secret message to me. He's testing me, asking me to meet him half way.

I postpone the tedious paper I was about to write about the Civil War, then spend the rest of the afternoon figuring out what to wear. I want to look cool, but casual. So all my dresses, including the polka-dotted blue one I wore today, are out. Of course, none of my jeans have been washed since my last shift at the gas station two days ago, but I don't think anyone will notice.

I decide on my favorite pair of jeans, my vintage smiley-face T-shirt with the eyes that land right on my boobs and make them look way bigger, and, of course, Johnny's cardigan. That will be my secret message back to him: Ask me. All you have to do is ask!

At dinner, I'm practically buzzing but my parents don't seem to notice. Every night, we eat during Jeopardy and I wash dishes during Wheel of Fortune while my mom spits out answers to the puzzles in a bored monotone. She's never wrong and almost always faster than the people on the show. My dad tells her every night she should go on TV and win us a bunch of money, but she says she has no use for Hollow-wood. (That's what she calls it.) I think she's afraid she'll freeze up. She probably would. The only place where she can really hold court is in this house. Everywhere else she's nothing.

My parents are nearly the opposite of each other. My dad is tall and fat and hairy where my mom is short and skinny with mousy brown hair that's so thin in places you can see through to her scalp.

We don't really talk to each other. We just stare at the blue glow of the TV, sitting just like we always do. My dad on the left side of the couch, my mom on the right. I'm on the old wooden rocking chair that I'm not allowed to creak. There are grooves in the couch shaped like each of them, but no groove shaped like me, just a smooth spot in the wood that could be anybody.

Sitting here, watching them transfixed by Alex Trebec, I want to share it with somebody. I want to scream: I'm going out with Johnny tonight!

It feels like they should notice the electricity racing over my skin. Maybe it's better they don't. It's a school night and there's no way they'll let me go if they know. So I stay quiet, letting the energy bounce through my fidgety legs until they're bumping against my TV tray and my mom glares at me to stop.

My appetite is revved up with all my excitement too, so I go back to the kitchen and take a second helping of mashed potatoes and the biggest slice of blueberry cobbler left in the pan.

"You must be going through a growth spurt," my mother says as I come back into the living room. Behind her eyes, the message is different: too fat, too fat, too fat. She's skinny no matter what she eats, but I got my dad's genes, which isn't fair on a girl. I'm not exactly fat, but I'm not exactly skinny either. At least not like her.

I don't finish the cobbler. Instead, I pretend I have a lot of homework and ask to be excused.

"Not before dishes, young lady."

"Yes, ma'am." That means I have to sit there and wait for everyone else to finish, which is unbearable. My mother seems to know this and takes her time chewing. I count her bites just to keep myself from screaming: eighty-seven for one piece of mushy meatloaf. The minute she swallows her last mouthful I jump up and swipe the plate from her lap, then grab my dad's, which was finished almost before we sat down. I race toward the kitchen.

"Never seen anybody so excited to do dishes," Dad says.

My mother eyes me with suspicion as I leave the room. Then my dad guffaws at somebody getting kicked in the nuts on a commercial about cashews, and they forget about me again.

I wash all the dishes by hand. My mom has always been too cheap to buy a dishwasher, even though we can afford it. We own a gas station right by the highway, but you'd never know it from the way our house looks. Nothing has been updated in years. Time stopped when my little sister died. Everything is almost exactly the same, especially her bedroom.

My dad never sets foot in the kitchen and doesn't have any reason to care about a dishwasher, so my mom always gets her way. That's about how it works when it comes to most things. I'm pretty sure she doesn't budge on the dishwasher because she likes to see me suffer. She's the kind of person who will punish herself just to punish you.

I scrub and scrub, the grit of the meatloaf pan getting caught under my nails, which I suddenly realize look awful. That's something else I'll need to do before I leave. But finally the dishes are clean, dry, and back in the cabinets.

I race upstairs, intent on giving myself a manicure. I want to touch Johnny with beautiful hands, not split-nailed, water-wrinkled ones.

I skip my parents' room, even though I bet there's tons of nail polish in there. If Mom caught me in her room, she'd ground me for a month. She'd probably accuse me of playing with those stupid teddy bears, which she stole from Milly's room and keeps on display in there. I hate them. They all stare at you like they could come to life at any moment and kill you. She thinks I want them for myself, but I don't. I hate even going in there.

So instead of going into their room, I dig around in the linen closet, looking for some lotion and a bottle of nail polish I'm pretty sure I saw once. Like everything else in the house that's behind closed doors, the closet is a mess. Out in the open, it's like someone with OCD lives here. But in the drawers? Under the beds? Things have been shoved on top of things, taking every available space, so I have to practically unpack it like a suitcase to get access to the back.

Eventually, I find what I'm looking for: a bottle of Mellow Mauve #4 that looks so old I think my mother must have bought it when she was a teenager. But it's all I've got so it will have to do.

I wash my hands and slather them with lotion, then use the pair of scissors I got in kindergarten to cut my nails short. The nail polish comes out lumpy on my thumb and my forefinger too, but there's nothing else to paint them with so what else am I supposed to do?

"Why are you doing your nails?" My mother stands at the door. Her footsteps are so light I never hear her when she walks up.

"Just wanted to," I say, twisting the lid back on the bottle. I'll have to finish them later.

"Is that even yours?"

"I found it in the closet."

"Found it, huh? And where do you suppose it came from? The magical nail polish fairy?"

"No ma'am."

"Hand it over."

I do.

"Things cost money, Greta. I don't think you appreciate that. The clothes on your back, the roof over your head, the food on your plate. All of it costs." She never cared about the cost of things when Milly was alive. She spoiled her rotten. But now? Everything has a price.

"I know," I say, keeping my voice contrite. I don't want to piss her off tonight.

"Do you? How much do you think this nail polish cost?"

I want to say about a dollar, considering how old it is, but I aim higher because it sounds like she wants to impress me with it. "Five dollars?"

"Seven." This must be a lie. She'd never spend half so much money on something like nail polish. But I know well enough to just let it go. I don't want to have her upset with me tonight.

"See, that's what I'm talking about. You don't know the value of things."

"I'm sorry," I say.

"Okay," she says, but she doesn't leave. "Thought you said you had a lot of homework?"

"I do."

"Then maybe you should be concentrating on that instead of your vanity."

"Yes, ma'am."

She finally goes, taking the polish with her. Now there's

only color on three fingers of my left hand. It looks even worse than it did before.

I try to scratch it off, but it's not dry yet. Dusty pink smears on my fingers and underneath my other nails. I look like a child left alone with markers.

I start to cry, thinking about Johnny, what he'll think of me if he sees me like this. Everything needs to be perfect. And it's not. It's so not.

7

LATER, AFTER I CRY MYSELF out, I search as quietly as possible for nail polish remover and find none. This is turning into a disaster. Why did I even try?

I head out to the garage and haul an old can of paint thinner off the shelf to rinse my hands. The polish goes away, but the paint thinner makes my hands dry and red and no matter how much I wash it, I can't get the smell out. I decide it's okay. I decide if anyone notices, I'll just tell them I was helping my dad paint.

After I get my hands as clean as I can, I sneak back into my room and change into my nightgown. I know Mom will come to check at lights out, nine o'clock sharp, as always, so I have to be ready. I open the window near my bed and leave it that way even though it's a little chilly. If I don't, my parents will hear the creak of its rise when I leave. I have to be careful. If they catch me sneaking out, I'll lose all my privileges and have to work extra shifts at the gas station until Christmas.

I barely tuck myself into bed before she opens the door, without knocking, of course.

"Little cold in here," my mom says. She's always cold.

"I like it," I say.

"Suit yourself," she says. "Say your prayers?"

"Yes, ma'am," I say, even though I didn't. I haven't talked to God for a long time.

"Goodnight then," my mom says. She leaves but doesn't close the door.

I wait two hours like that. Eyes wide open, listening for them to fall asleep. It's hard because the television is always on in their room. They go to sleep with it on and it plays until morning. Tonight, it seems extra loud. I can't tell if it's my dad's snoring I hear or a TV show about cops shooting gangsters. But after a while, I decide I can't wait any longer. The movie will start in an hour and it will take forty-five minutes to bike there if I bike as fast as I can.

I slip out of bed and slip off my nightgown. Then I tug my jeans on and put on my T-shirt and wrap myself up in Johnny's sweater. It smells exactly like him. He smells like no one else in the world—like baby powder and cloves and pine needles. I tug the sweater to my nose and inhale. It immediately makes me smile. Nothing else matters. Not my mom, not my fingernails, not my smelly hands. Nothing. All that matters is I'm going to see him.

I wonder what he'll say when he sees me? He'll be so surprised, so happy!

Our house is a ranch style, so I don't have to worry about

hurting myself to get out the window. I slide out onto the porch, feeling lucky my bedroom is near the front of the house.

CREAK.

My first step is so loud I almost jump but catch myself at the last second. I stand still, as still as I possibly can, and listen. And listen. And listen. I count sixty Mississippis until I'm sure a full minute has passed without hearing anything.

It's a short walk off the porch, but I take my time after that, testing every step for squeaks before I put my full weight on it. Eventually, I make it to where my bike is propped against the porch rails out front. I wheel it out our long, dusty driveway.

Our house isn't the greatest, but we have lots of land, which most people out there would call a waste because we don't raise cattle on it or farm it or anything. It just runs wild. Well, kind of wild. It's mostly prairie grasses and dust and tumbleweeds, which don't get too wild. And there's a stream that runs through it, which is rare out here. There's a snake pit too—a magnificent display of nature's teeming power—but I try not to go over there anymore. It can be dangerous.

This land was where my mom grew up and my parents like their space. They don't want nosy neighbors or loud parties or lots of cars, so we live on the outskirts of a town called Prairie Grove. It's barely big enough to call itself a town, made up of just a smattering of truck stops and fast food joints on a vast expanse of plains a couple hours north of Denver. Gas sells anywhere, I guess.

At the end of the long driveway, I stop again and look back to make sure no one's there. All the lights are off. A blue flicker glows from my parent's room near the back, but it's the only light on in our house. And our house is the only one on the prairie until the Jenkins' two miles down the road.

I hop on my bike and peddle as fast as I can, letting the wind whip a smile on my face. The air is crisp, but not yet too cold. It's only October 16th and Colorado doesn't usually get a first snow on the plains until after Halloween. In other words, it's perfect outside.

I feel magical, weightless and free, my long red hair whipping behind me like a flame. My mother thinks haircuts are a waste of money for girls and I think she's right. My hair is gorgeous, longer than anyone else in my class. It goes all the way down to my waist and is my best feature.

I imagine what Johnny's face would look like if he were riding next to me. I imagine him staring at my beauty, at my hair blowing in the wind. He'd be totally transfixed, so distracted he could barely keep his bike straight. I pump my legs hard. The harder I ride, the sooner I can see him.

There's only one theater nearby, a small one in the Prairie Grove town center. I make it there in forty-three minutes flat, a personal record. There's a crowd lined up outside for the midnight showing of Z-Force, but I don't see Johnny. Suddenly I feel panicky. What if he's not here?

What if he drove to the nicer theater in Ft. Collins, or even all the way out to Denver to see it on the big screen?

Then, I hear it. His laugh. His laugh is magical, like bubbles coming up from a hot spring. I turn my head to look and see him coming around the block behind me, surrounded by some other kids from my school. My heart lights up. I shove my bike into the bike stand and rush over to him.

"Hi, Johnny!" I said. "I made it!"

He turns to me and his face goes blank for a moment. I don't understand. Doesn't he want me there? Didn't he post that message especially so I would see it?

Recognition dawns on his face. Maybe he's trying to play it cool. "Greta, right? You come out to see the Force?"

"Be there or suffer the wrath of Zelon!" I say enthusiastically.

He looks confused for a second. A tall guy next to him says, "Your post, dude."

Then Johnny says, "Right. Of course. Facebook." Something odd flashes across his face before he smiles and says, "Don't want any lightning rays to the heart, right?"

"Right," I say, even though I know nothing at all about Z-Force, only that *he* was so excited about it.

"Well, enjoy the show," he says, walking right past me with his friends.

A girl I barely know named Mindy, the president of the drama club, grabs his hand. It's the hand I should be holding. She looks over her shoulder at me as she says to

Johnny, "Isn't that your sweater?"

"I dunno," Johnny says. Of course he knows. Of course he had to remember giving it to me. It was like a moment in a movie. It was *our* moment.

"She smells like the gas station," Mindy said. "You'd think they could afford a shower."

They go inside without me. *That girl.* Stupid little actress bitch. I do not like *that girl.*

8

I DON'T WATCH THE MOVIE. I grab my bike and head straight home, peddling slower this time, not paying attention to where I'm going. I'm so stupid. Stupid and dumb and useless and ugly. Of course Johnny has a girlfriend. Of course he does. He's perfect and I'm just another lame girl who wants to be his.

Now *that girl* has him brainwashed against me. How will I ever break through to him? This whole thing is her fault.

My pace picks up and I'm going faster than I've ever gone before. My thighs ache and my feet burn from the pressure against the pedals. I have to do better. I have to be better. I have to do better. I have to be better.

I round a turn at top speed. There's a loud honk and I veer to the side just in time to miss a pickup truck. The adjustment sends me flying into the bank. I hit a rock and tumble over my handlebars.

My breath is gone. My life is gone. I should have just let the truck hit me. My hands arc in the dirt and I'm screaming and pounding the earth.

My chest heaves up and down, pumping like the pistons of an engine. My fingernails pull and crack. My knuckles redden against the rocks.

Dirt mists into the air around me, making the moon dim behind a brown cloud and settling on my face and clothes. All I see is black, black, black. All I see is the face of *that girl*, that nasty, nasty girl.

Then I see something else—a tall shadow, black against the moonlight. The driver of the truck.

"You okay, honey?" He's older, maybe forty, with a thick layer of mud across his boots. A rancher, probably hired help. I've never seen him before. Looking over I see his truck is rusted out at places, a product of the stuff they put all over the roads when it snows.

I swipe at my eyes. "I'm fine." I pick up my bike and wheel it off in the opposite direction. One wheel is bent, lopsided off the axle, and makes a *thunk-thunk-thunk* noise against the dirt as it rolls.

"Hey, hold on there. I'm real sorry about that. Let me at least give you a ride."

I stop and turn to face him. "You were driving really fast, you know."

"And you were riding against the flow in the wrong lane."

We stare each other down, both right.

"Come on. You aren't getting anywhere on that thing tonight."

I don't say anything. Riding in cars with strangers is as

off limits as it comes, but he's right about the bike. It would take me hours to guide the thing back home and I'm exhausted. I'm half tempted to head back to town and call my dad for a ride, but there's still a chance they don't have to know about this. I've had about as much as I can handle for one day.

He takes my silence as consent and hefts my bike into the bed of his truck, then goes around to open the door for me. At least he's a gentleman.

I get inside and tell him where to go. He pulls out a flask and hands it to me.

"You look pretty shook up. This might help."

I start to protest that I'm not twenty-one, only sixteen, but then realize he must think I'm of age, or he wouldn't have offered it in the first place. It makes me feel better. I'm a woman in his eyes, not a stupid little girl. I find myself untwisting the cap and taking a long swig, trying not to grimace. It's the first time I've ever tasted the stuff and it stings.

"Thatta girl," he says.

I take a deep breath and let the liquid heat my throat as it drops toward my stomach. I take another long gulp, feeling smoother, calmer already. It was sweet of him to give it to me. It was exactly what I needed.

"What's your name?" he asks.

"Greta," I say.

"That's a real pretty name. Unique."

I like the way he's looking at me. Like it's not just my

name that's pretty.

"Thanks," I say, reaching out for his hand. He seems surprised, but he doesn't pull away. I can feel the swirl of the liquor in my belly. It's making me bold.

I take my hand out of his and put it on his thigh. Then farther up until I'm touching what I've never touched before.

He pulls over.

He tugs my shirt over my head. Then my bra is off and my jeans are down and his rough hands scrape over my bare, creamy skin.

He doesn't seem to care that I call him Johnny.

The next morning when I get online to check Johnny's profile, I can't see it. I try everything, but all I can see is his photo and name. His statuses are gone. His favorite movies, favorite bands. All of it. I click the little box that says ADD AS FRIEND, hoping it was a mistake.

But it doesn't feel like a mistake, it feels like a punishment. He knows, he knows, he knows.

He couldn't know, could he? He couldn't have seen it. I'm sure we were alone.

But maybe he felt it. We are connected in a way that's hard to understand. Maybe he could feel me pulling away from him, a fray in the rope that ties us to one another.

I wasn't unfaithful to you, I want to tell him. Not in my heart.

But before I can type anything, before I can send him a

message to let him know the real truth, my mom walks into my bedroom without knocking. She's holding the broom like it's her scepter.

"Where were you last night?" she asks, her mouth ruler-straight and concrete-solid.

"In bed," I say, even though I can tell she knows. Somehow she knows.

"I saw your bike. It wasn't like that yesterday."

Shit.

"I think somebody must have pulled into our driveway and hit it."

"You're a little liar, Greta. You always have been. But you're too stupid to know how bad you are at it. Bend over."

I know what's coming—it's happened so many times before—but I can't take it. Not today. Not after everything that happened last night.

"Please, Momma," I beg, tears springing to my eyes. "I just wanted to go out with my friends."

"Lie," she says, a light in her eyes that scares me. "You have no friends. Bend over."

I cry harder.

"Am I gonna have to make you?" my mom asks. "Because I will."

There's no use fighting her. I've tried. She wins every time. Somehow, she always wins.

All I want is to be alone, so I decide it's best to just get it over with. I pull down my pajama pants and my underwear and place my hands on the bed.

She swings the broom like it's a bat. She doesn't stop even when I scream, even when I'm crawling away from her, even when my face is so wet with tears I think I might drown. The only thing that ever satisfies her is watching me bleed.

Part Four

My Blake

9

BY THE END OF THE next day, Amber's already gotten invitations to five parties that night, and I've gotten two. We strategize about which one we'll go to. There are a couple low-key things in the dorm, one down the hall and one upstairs. There's a floor-party the RA is hosting, that we're supposedly all invited to, but I had to hear about it from Amber. There's a big thing at some frat house and a thing at a bar. We decide to try and make an appearance at all of them.

I am so excited I can hardly stand it. My skin feels electric. I've never been to a party before, not for real, and tonight there will be five. Five!

Amber helps me decide what to wear. As we page through my closet, it suddenly dons on me how slim the selection is. Amber's wardrobe bursts with clothes but mine is sparse. I've been shopping all summer, but I didn't realize how many outfits it takes to be a girl like Amber. I really need to get a job.

Amber is wearing an electric blue minidress that pops off her tan skin and blond hair and seems to force you to look straight into her huge blue eyes. It's stunning and there's no way I'll look as good as her. No way. I start to panic a little.

"I don't think I have anything," I say. "Maybe we should go shopping." I still haven't bought any books.

"I have an idea."

She goes to her own closet and pulls out a dress. It is red as lips and looks too tiny for my body. Like a tube sock.

"You should wear this. With your fair skin, it'll be perfect. Trust me. I'm basically an expert shopper. I almost went to fashion school, but really, where's that gonna go?"

"I'm not sure it will fit."

She eyes me up and down. "It will. Just give it a try."

I take off my clothes and Amber looks away. Maybe I should have gone to the bathroom to change. I pull the dress over my head and tug it down. It hugs every part of my body. I would never choose something like this for myself so I ignore how I have to pull it down over my thighs and try not to think about how much smaller her hips are than mine.

"You look hot," she says.

"I do?"

"Smokin', baby."

I look in the mirror. She's right. I do look hot. The effect is crazy. Just one dress, and all my flesh is sucked into a perfect hourglass shape. My cleavage is insane.

"Can I try something with your hair?"

"Sure." The question is so normal I want to cry. It's just like how the other girls used to talk to each other in high school. "I'd love that."

Amber smiles and races to the bathroom. She comes back with a brush and slicks my wild mane back into a tight topknot. I look at least ten years older. Sophisticated and modern. It actually looks like I could be Amber's friend. I don't know what to say.

"It's perfect," she says. "I've wanted to pull all that hair off your face since I met you. You have incredible cheekbones. You should show them off."

I reach up to touch my cheekbones, suddenly seeing what she sees. I can't stop staring at myself.

"Thanks."

Amber pulls a bottle out from under her bed with a sly look. It's Peach Schnapps. "Daddy snuck it to me before he left."

I want to show her how surprised I am that her dad lets her drink, but I don't think it would be cool. It would spoil the moment. Maybe all cool girls' parents let them drink.

"My dad lets me drink too," I say.

"Oh yeah?" she looks a little confused. Surprised too.

"Uh huh. All the time."

"I thought you said your parents were strict?"

"They are. But they don't care about drinking."

"Cool, whatever. Anyway," she lifts the bottle, "To college!" she says. Then she takes a big swig and hands the bottle to me.

"To college!" I say. My throat burns and I try not to cough, but I can't help it. Amber laughs at me and tugs me out the door. We leave the bottle sitting out on her desk like it's no big deal at all and race out into the night.

The welcome party in the lounge is so lame. Everyone is playing a game where they're tossing a balloon to each other. It's moving so slow in the air it makes them look like they belong on the short bus. I'm not sure what the point of it is. Amber takes one look at the whole setup, grabs my arm, and makes me keep walking straight through to the front door. A guy waves at her as we pass, our RA I think, but she pretends not to see him. We bust out laughing when we get outside.

"Did you see Tom?" she says.

"Oh my god yes. I thought you didn't!"

"Oh, I saw him. But there's no way we were going to that party. We would have been stuck there all night."

"Right?" I have no idea why she thinks so, though. Maybe it was because of the balloon game. I thought it looked dumb too, but I don't know much about parties.

"I could feel the lame all over me. I didn't want to catch it," she says.

"I know!" I say. I didn't know.

"Shit," she says, looking behind her.

"What? Is he coming out to talk to us?" I whirl around to look at the front doors, but don't see anyone there.

"No. I just realized there are two more parties back

inside."

"Ohmygod." I say it like Amber says it, like it's one word.

She straightens up and takes a deep breath, ready to go back inside.

"Wait," I say, grabbing her arm this time. "Back door."

"You're a genius."

I am a genius!

10

THE NEXT PARTY IS DOWN the hall from our room and only has six people at it. They're lounging around on the floor playing video games and drinking beer. The guy who invited us, Tucker, gives us a look that seems to say he's sorry. Tucker has sandy hair and the belly of someone who has had experience drinking even though his face looks like a baby's.

He whispers something in Amber's ear that makes her laugh. Amber grabs my arm again and whispers into my ear. "Just play along."

"I'm gonna go help these guys move some furniture," Tucker says. "We'll be back." The guy who is probably his roommate gives him a "whatever dude" look and waves to him as we walk out. No one thinks we'll be back. I don't know why he had to tell the lie to leave. It didn't really seem like they wanted us there either.

"Oh my God," Tucker says. "Thank you. You have literally saved me from the most boring night of my life."

How we "literally" saved him I don't know.

He grabs Amber's face and kisses her right on the mouth as a joke, then does the same to me, too. It's supposed to be funny, but I think he likes it, likes kissing us like that, like he owns a little part of us, now—a little part of both of us.

I don't like the kiss, but Amber doesn't seem to mind. She laughs and smacks him on the arm, so I laugh too. I don't tell anyone it's the first time I've been kissed, at least like this, from a boy my own age.

"You guys are literally my knights in shining armor right now. I totally owe you. What do you want to do now? We can do whatever you guys want. I'm your slave for the night. Or forever if you want. That's how much I owe you."

"I heard about another party upstairs," Amber says. "Let's go check that out."

"Perfect," he says. Then he offers us his elbows, "Ladies?"

Amber rolls her eyes but hooks her arm into his. I do the same on his left arm and we walk back to the elevator.

"So, you guys got boyfriends back home?" Ohmygod. Does he think we're hot? Is this guy into us? I think he must be. Why else would he be asking if we had boyfriends? No one has ever asked me that before. Then I realize who I'm with—the blond goddess. He's probably just asking about Amber.

"Sort of," Amber says, which I think means she's not into Tucker because she told me herself she didn't have a boyfriend.

Tucker turns to me, "How about you?"

So, not just Amber. Me too. He's into me too.

"Yeah," I say, following Amber's lead. "I have a boyfriend. Sorry."

"You girls are killing me here."

"I think you'll survive," Amber says. Then she looks at me and rolls her eyes again. She must be used to getting attention from guys like this, guys beneath her level.

The elevator dings and opens onto nineteen. Amber leans over to look at me, "Third time's a charm?"

"God, I hope so." This makes them both laugh. I feel alive.

We walk up to the door. It's wide open, but dark inside. There's music playing, some sexy, low R&B beat filling up the whole hallway.

Tucker taps on the door as we walk inside, "Hello?"

No one says anything. The first thing I see is a guy in a corner with a bottle. He doesn't seem to notice us. He's staring at the bunk beds across the room.

I turn to see what he's looking at, and I see skin. Lots of it. On each of the bunk beds, there's a couple making out. The couple on the bottom bunk is practically naked. So is the couple above them. As the couple on the top bunk rolls, another girl appears behind them, joining in, three people in one bed.

"Oh, my stars and stripes!" Amber gasps. She races out of the room with Tucker.

"Did you see that?! What was that?!" Tucker says.

"How could you not see it?" Amber says.

I hear their voices from the hallway, but I can't move. I can't even look away. I want to absorb everything I'm seeing, this tangle of bodies as it writhes together, until I understand it, until I can comprehend why. It's not that they're beautiful. They're not. It's that they're together. These people chose to be together this way, and I don't understand why.

"Greta!" It's Amber's voice, calling me from the hallway, but still I don't move. "Greta, come on!"

The boy on the top bunk sits up and stares at me as the two girls keep kissing him. They're all over him, rubbing and feeling and kissing his body and suddenly it's all too much. It's too much love for one person. He shouldn't be allowed all of that. Some of us have none and this boy gets more than his fair share. It's not right. And his eyes are still on me, daring me to watch, daring me to join them, maybe. This boy doesn't deserve it. He's no Johnny. Not even close. He's a wolf and I am Little Red.

My face twists in anger. I want to tear him off the bed. I take a step forward and reach up toward the bunk to hoist myself up to him, but just as I do, Amber grabs my hand and yanks me back toward the door.

"What are you doing? Come on."

We burst into the hall. "What was that in there?" Amber asks.

"Nothing, I—"

"You wanted in on it, didn't you?" Tucker says, laughing.

He's making fun of me, his eyes bulging and electric, his stupid fat baby face wrinkled up in a stupid smile plastered on his stupid middle-aged salesman body.

"Ohmygod-Ohmygod-Ohmygod-Ohmygod!" Amber says, laughing. "Please tell me you weren't gonna join in."

"No, I didn't. I wasn't going to—"

"I saw you. You were climbing up into that bed," Tucker says through heaves of laughter, "You were gonna get all up in that shit." He's laughing so hard he's bent over now.

"No, I wasn't."

Amber's just staring, her mouth wide open in a huge grin. She thinks it's funny too, but something inside her holds back from laughing like Tucker. Something inside her hesitates.

"Yes, you were. You dirty little dog! You must be so horny!" He can't catch his breath he's laughing so hard. "Ugh! That is so disgusting."

"Shut up!" I yell. "Shut the fuck up!" I race toward the stairwell.

"Awe, don't run away, sweetie! I was just fucking with you!" Tucker says to my back.

"Shut up," Amber says to Tucker. "Greta, wait!"

I slam through the stairwell door. My heels clang on the metal stairs as I pound my way down, flight after flight after flight. The sound makes a trail of echoes that drowns out Amber & Tucker's voices behind me.

I reach my floor and burst through, racing toward my room. I want to crawl under my blanket and hide forever and never talk to anyone ever again, but when I get to the door, I realize I didn't bring my keys. Amber was carrying hers for both of us. She has them in her purse.

The actual awkwardness of the college experience settles in on me for maybe the first time. Will I ever have time to myself again? Will I ever be alone?

Amber and Tucker come through the door together and I turn away from them and swipe at the tears on my cheeks. I can't let them see me cry. I won't let them see me cry. But Tucker grabs my shoulders and turns me to look me in the face before I can pull myself together.

"Hey," Tucker says, "Aw, don't cry. I'm really sorry. Fuck, I'm such an asshole. I wasn't being serious. I was just messing with you. I swear."

"Go away," I say, pulling away from his grasp.

"Tucker, just—" Amber sighs, "just give us a minute, okay?" She puts an arm around my shoulder and pulls out her keys. "Let's get you cleaned up."

"I really am sorry," Tucker says. As the door closes in his face, I break down.

"Hey, it's okay. It's okay. It's not a big deal, okay? Just calm down. Take a deep breath."

"I wasn't going to do it," I sob. My makeup is probably ruined. "I wasn't going to do those things with them."

"Okay. I know. We were just teasing you. That's all. We took it too far."

"I wouldn't ever do something like that. That's disgusting."

"I know," Amber says. She lets me catch my breath before she asks, "but what were you doing? It really looked like you were climbing up there."

I panic and say the first thing that comes to mind. "I was just—I've never seen anything like that before. And they didn't even notice we were there. I sort of wanted to see how close I could get and then yell 'boo!' or something."

"Ohmygod. That would have been hilarious."

"Yeah," I smile through my tears.

"No wonder you looked like you were concentrating so hard."

"Did I?"

"Yeah. It was like you had laser eyes."

I laugh and wipe away the tears. "I feel so stupid. I'm such a baby."

"No, you're not. I cry all the time. This summer I cried when I accidentally stepped on a worm. Can you imagine that? An eighteen-year-old woman crying 'cause she killed a worm? Now that's being a baby."

She laughs and it makes me laugh and before I know it my face is clean and I have a new layer of mascara on and she's convinced me to go to another party. This one is at a frat house. I almost decided not to, but she's right—I will feel better if I put the worst part of the night behind me. She really is my best friend.

Before we go, she grabs the bottle of Schnapps. "I think we might need a little liquid courage for the road. What do you say?"

"Oh yeah."

11

TUCKER HAS A CAR AND offers to drive us all to the frat house. He knows somebody there; his older brother pledged SigUp at a different school and graduated a couple years ago. There's still tension between us, but he's trying to smooth over how much of an asshole he was to me. I haven't yet decided if I'll forgive him. Probably not. Right now, it feels nice to let him beg.

The Schnapps is helping too. I'm sipping at it in the back seat, letting it warm me and tingle through my veins. The buzz in my belly feels like magic. I press my hand against the window as the passing lights dance on the glass.

"I sort of double owe you guys now, for being such an asshole. So I'll be your extra slave. It'll be tough, but I think I can pull it off."

Amber giggles. "What's an extra slave?"

"Oh, you know, book carrying, public humiliation, sexual favors. Your basic routine."

"Wowie. You don't ever stop, do you?" she says.

"Never had a good enough reason to." He smiles wide and I suddenly realize his smile is charming. It's what makes him pull off all that swagger in a body that's less than handsome. If he weren't smiling, it wouldn't work.

"Your smile is charming," I say. The words feel like they're coming from a foggy part of my brain.

"Why, thank you." He turns to Amber, whose eyes are bulging out of her face at my boozy compliment. "See, she gets what I'm laying down."

"I said your smile is charming, I didn't say the rest of you is charming." The alcohol has made me bold.

"Burn!" Amber yells, laughing. I laugh too. So does Tucker.

"I guess I deserved that."

We pass by a huge, white mansion with tall columns supporting a wide upper balcony that spans the length of the house. Music is thumping from inside and there are big Greek letters hanging from the roof.

"You guys planning to pledge?" I don't know what he means, but Amber answers right away.

"I am. Are you?" she says to Tucker.

"I think so. SigUp seems pretty good, that's where my brother went, but so does Phi Zeta. Not sure which one I'm leaning toward yet."

"I don't really have a choice. My momma was a Kappa Kappa Nu, so that means I'm obligated."

"Listen to that cute little accent of yours." Tucker's voice gets all high-pitched and southern. "My momma was a

Kappa, so I'm gonna be one too." He laughs.

Amber punches him in the arm.

"Owe!"

"Never make fun of a southern woman. Our daddies teach us how to punch."

"Jeez, sorry."

"Rush starts next week, right?" she asks.

"I think so. How about you, Greta? You gonna pledge?"

"Uh, yeah, I think so." Amber turns around in her seat to look at me.

"Please say you'll pledge Kappa? I don't know anyone there yet and all my mom's sisters' daughter's I've met have been super bitchy. I'm actually dreading it."

"Okay," I say, excited, and pass her the bottle.

"Thank goodness. I think I'd just die if I had to walk into those meet-n-greets alone."

"I'm sure you'll do fine," Tucker says. "Two pretty girls like you?"

"You don't know the first thing about me Tucker Holten," Amber says. "Not the first thing. For all you know I could be a serial killer."

"Are you a serial killer?"

"I might be."

"No, you're not."

"Maybe not, but I might as well be when it comes to stuffy get-togethers like that. I just can't help myself from sticking my foot in my mouth every chance I get. It'll be a miracle if I make it in."

"They basically have to let you in if you're a legacy," Tucker says.

"Which will make it a hundred times worse if I mess it up and don't get in."

I don't get it. What's the big deal? It's just a club. But if Amber's this worried about getting in, maybe I should be too.

"You'll get in," he says.

"What, you can see the future now too?" she says. "Oh! There it is."

Amber points to another frat house. This one is red brick and stately with vines climbing toward a black metal roof. There are huge Greek letters mounted to the brick, painted white to pop against the red. And more music cranking from inside, so loud the party could be on the street.

"Drop us off out front," Amber says. "My feet hurt enough already in these shoes. Sometimes it's a burden being a girl."

"You're a bossy little thing, aren't you?"

"I thought you said you were our slave for the night?"

"As you command, my lady."

He drops us off out front. We leave the bottle in the car, but I can feel the sway it has on me with every step.

"So you like Tucker, huh?" Amber asks, girly and smiling and gossipy.

"Tucker's an asshole."

"But you like him? I mean, I've liked plenty of assholes in my day. Sometimes that's the allure, isn't it?"

"No. I don't like him. I just said his smile was charming. Like 'snake charmer' charming, not 'prince charming' charming."

"You sure? 'Cause it kind of seemed like you liked him."

"Not even a little bit. Let's go meet some real men." I said the last thing because it sounds like something I'm supposed to say—something she would say.

"Now you're talking."

It doesn't occur to me until then how we're going to get inside. There's a big guy standing guard at the door who looks like he's there for the sole purpose of telling people to go away. But it doesn't turn out to be a problem. The guy out front takes one look at the two of us and smiles.

"Welcome to SigUp, ladies." He opens the door. "Have a good night."

I can't believe it.

Amber sneaks a knowing smile at me. I think it means we're looking hot. Everything in me buzzes at the idea. They let us in. Just like that. They let us in.

We walk through the door into another world. The place looks like a nightclub stuffed inside a mansion. There are people. So many people. Everyone is dressed like either a geek or a Greek, some in tiny togas that barely cover anything. Some in slutty schoolgirl skirts and black glasses. We didn't know about the theme, so we sort of stand out.

We step into another room, a bigger room, and there's a crush of bodies dancing close, short-skirted and grinding against each other. Palms grab asses. Chests rub against each other. Lips touch.

Amber raises her arms to dance. "Yeah! Now this is what I'm talking about."

Then she grabs my hand and tugs me into the crowd. But it's too much all at once. The booze is sloshing around in my tummy, making me feel like I have the flu. I break away from her grasp and find a restroom in the hall where I can vomit.

I gag it all out into the toilet, one big yellow mess, and my stomach feels better.

When I come out, Tucker is there waiting for me, holding a red plastic solo cup full of who-knows-what.

"So you like my smile, huh?"

"Jesus, just forget I said that, okay?"

"Okay," he says. I think he's going to let me go find Amber, but then he grabs me by the arm and presses me against the wall and kisses me, shoving his tongue through my lips.

I want to bite it. I open my mouth wide to snap, but he pulls away before I can. He coughs, gags.

"Oh my God," he says. "Did you just puke?"

"You're the one who kissed me, asshole."

"You're a weird little bitch, you know that?"

The tears prick at my eyes, but I try to summon Amber, try to think what she would say. "Go fuck yourself."

Then I slap him across the face like in an old-fashioned movie.

"What the fuck?" he says.

My hand is on fire, but it feels good. I don't say anything else, don't answer the shocked question in his eyes. I just walk away like I'm a queen. I am.

It's then I realize I'm not doing what I always do in a crowd. I'm not looking for Johnny. It's the first time I've ever realized I'm not doing it, and I panic all of a sudden. Could I have missed him somewhere along the way? When was the last time I looked for him? What does it mean?

I look around frantically, as though the very realization I should look means he will be there, he must be there. But as I scan the room, I don't see Johnny. I see someone else.

I see Blake.

I see him for the first time and my whole life changes in that instant. All thoughts of Johnny go away. They disappear, burned up in the heat of him.

He walks toward me like he can feel it too—feel our connection. But instead of stopping, he walks right by. I turn and see him approach Amber.

Isn't it funny how the most insignificant decisions can have the biggest consequences? If I hadn't gone to the restroom that night, if Tucker hadn't kissed me or Amber hadn't had that bottle of Schnapps, maybe Blake would have seen me first. And maybe Amber wouldn't have had to die.

12

AMBER AND BLAKE DANCE TOGETHER all night.

I stay close to them, batting away offers to dance and random gyrating dudes and drinks sloshed in my direction. I never knew how annoying it was to be pretty.

The party thins out, couples tugging each other into secret corners and the bedrooms upstairs, others leaving altogether.

I'm against a wall watching them. He has his hands on her waist and her arms are exactly where mine would be—around his neck. He has such a lovely neck, strong and corded and long. Amber has to stretch up all the way on her tiptoes because he's so tall. He should be with someone who doesn't have to reach—someone taller—someone like me.

A slow song comes on and he pulls her even closer—as if that's even possible. There's no space between them, but I want to slide into the absence of it to wedge them apart. He leans down to kiss her. She sags her weight into his arms like she's not standing at all, like all the energy she had a moment ago was swept away by the force of him. But he holds her tight. She doesn't need muscles. She doesn't need legs.

His hand moves down across her ass, so low he's sliding it under the hem of her dress and up again until the whole room can see her panties. He looks up to see who's watching, but I'm the only one. He holds my eyes.

This is what I'll do to you, he's telling me. *If I had seen you first, it would have been you.*

He can probably tell she's my friend, which makes things difficult for both of us. Very difficult. And he's loyal, I can tell. He wouldn't want to embarrass her by leaving her alone to be with me.

I smile at him, *she'll understand,* I say with my gaze. *Everyone can understand true love.*

Then he turns back to Amber and whispers something in her ear. She looks over her shoulder at me, then says something back to him and comes over.

"You'll be okay if I leave you here for a little bit, right?"

"Where are you going?"

"Nowhere," she says with a sly smile. "It's okay. You don't have to worry about me."

"Okay," I say.

She grins and prances back to Blake, who takes her hand and leads her toward the stairs. He looks back to me with a smile as he walks her up. *It should have been you. All of this should have been you.*

When they cross up into the floor above, I follow. At the

top of the steps, I see them disappear behind a door. Blake's door, probably.

I sit down next to it and press my ear against the door. I hear them right away. I know what they're doing because I've made those noises before. He's making her moan and my body responds to the sound of it—to the energy of him behind that door. I imagine it's me. I imagine his hands on me, imagine myself so overcome by his touch that I'm making the same sounds she does. My hand drifts down to stop the ache between my legs.

Oh, Blake.

Oh, Blake.

Oh, Blake.

13

A FOOT NUDGES ME AWAKE. I'm still outside his room, but the sounds of the party are silent. Light beams in from a window down the hall.

"Hey. Time to go home, honey."

"Huh?" My breath is sour and my thoughts are foggy.

"You gotta go. It's morning."

The foot belongs to a tall guy with messy blond hair. He's wearing a CU T-shirt over boxers. I can see him bobbing inside them like a buoy.

"My friend's in there."

"Wake her up if you want to, but you gotta go."

I get to my feet and tap on the door. "Amber?"

The guy just stands there, watching me. Like I'm lying or something. I knock harder.

"Amber?"

The door opens and it's Blake. He's completely naked and the sight of him makes me lose my breath. He's got the kind of body statues are modeled after. Every bit of him is chiseled and perfect, even his sleep-mashed hair.

"Oh, it's you," he says to me.

"Jeez man," the hall guy says, looking away.

"You're the one who knocked," Blake grins.

"This girl says her friend's in there."

Blake cracks the door wider and I catch a peek at his enormous room. It must be the biggest in the house. Behind him, I see Amber sit up, lifting the sheet to cover herself.

"Greta? What are you still doing here?"

Everyone is staring at me now, waiting on me for something.

"I was just—I just woke up."

"I'm okay. You can go home."

"Right, okay."

The door closes and I hear Amber say, "Sorry."

I walk back to the dorm, but Amber has the keys, so I go to the lounge instead of our room and fall asleep on the couch.

Amber finds me in the lounge and is really sorry, especially when she feels me glare at her like I want her to die.

I want her to die.

"Seriously, I totally forgot you didn't have keys. I feel really bad."

She looks at me like it's my turn to say it's okay. I really don't want to say it's okay.

"Can you forgive me, Greta? Please?

Her eyes look sad as a puppy's, and I hate that. What am

I supposed to do? I don't care about the keys. It's not the keys at all. And the rest? Is it her fault? Is the thing between them serious enough to worry about at all? It couldn't last. He had to have felt me there.

"Okay. Fine."

She grips me in a huge hug. "I'm so sorry. That was so shitty of me. I'll never do it again, I swear. You hungry? I think the cafeteria is still serving lunch. Why don't we get something to eat? I have so much to tell you. Like, so much."

We go to the cafeteria, still in our smeared mascara and dresses from last night. Lots of people stare as we walk in. Most of them seem like nerdy types and must be jealous we were out partying so late.

The cafeteria looks like the food court at the mall, lots of different stalls where you can get any kind of food you want. Bright colors, slick floors, big windows with views of the courtyard that sits at the center of all the dorms on the west campus.

We get our trays and sit down. Amber's having two big slices of pizza, a brownie, and small dish of macaroni and cheese. I'm having a salad. Her pizza smells so good. Salty and tangy and cheesy. All that cheese! But if I ate what she ate my silhouette would balloon out farther than Marilyn Monroe's dress. She gets everything I want.

"So," she says. "What happened with you last night? You find anyone to make you forget about Johnny?"

Her grin is so sly it makes me sick. I want to tell her that, no, I didn't. I want to tell her some people are faithful, some people understand true love isn't just an item on a drive-through menu. But then I remember Blake.

It's different, I decide. Very different.

"Maybe," I say.

"Really? What's his name? Did I meet him?"

"No." It's not a lie. She couldn't have met him, not really. Not the real him. Only I know him that way.

"So? What's he like?"

I look at her, my smile just as sly. "Gorgeous," I say, a grin spreading across my face. "And smart. And sweet. So sweet."

"Greta Bell! You little hoe bag!"

"Excuse me?"

"I mean, that was pretty fast," she says through big chews of pizza. "I thought you loved Johnny. *Loved* him."

"I do. I mean, I did. It's—I don't know. I thought I did, but now I realize I didn't even know what love was."

"Whoa. That sounds serious. You really like this guy, huh?"

"When you know, you know."

She grins big, then says. "I still get to call you a hoe bag."

"Like you have room to talk," I say, a little angrier than I want to sound.

"Never said I wasn't," she says. Then she stands on her chair and yells, "Attention everyone! Attention, please! I, Amber Renae Benedict, am officially a hoe bag!"

There are only a handful of people in the cafeteria, but

they all cheer. I can't help but to grin. She bows to the crowd, then sits down.

"Feel better now?" she says. "We're hoe bags together."

"Yes," I say. And I do.

But it's confusing to not be mad at her anymore. What happens when you love two people, but you can't love them both together?

I decide to talk to her about it.

"So, how was it last night?"

"Oh, you know. He was a guy."

"Are you going to see him again?"

"Him? I doubt it. I'm on the buffet plan, remember?"

My heart soars. It is possible. I can love them both at once. I stand up and give Amber a huge hug.

"What was that for?" she says, her face amused.

"Just because," I say. "I'm happy we get to be roommates."

"Me too," she says. "Now please, sit down and eat one of these slices. My eyes, as usual, were bigger than my stomach."

I snatch the slice off her plate and take a big bite.

First things first. When Amber crashes into her bed and falls asleep, I write Blake a note. Everyone says you're supposed to play hard to get, so I keep it simple:

Dear Blake,

It's okay now. Amber understands. We can be together. Come to me when you dare.

Sincerely,

Your One True Love

I go to the SigUp house and slide it into the mail slot, then leave before anyone sees me. He will be so excited.

14

ALL MY CLASSES ARE ON Mondays and Wednesdays. Which makes Tuesdays and Thursdays all for homework or whatever I want. It's strange, having all this free time. So different from high school.

On Tuesday, I go out to find a job. I put in applications at the student career center and then drive around Culford, trying to decide where else to look. Anywhere but a gas station, I decide. Anywhere but there.

I put in applications at an ice cream place and an old-fashioned burger diner where the waitresses wear roller skates. I hope I get hired there. That would be fun.

I decide to hang out at the diner for a minute and read some of my Biology textbook. The milkshake menu alone is so tempting I can barely keep myself from ordering all of them. I decide on a raspberry swirl malt and settle in.

And wouldn't you know it, not five minutes after my malt is delivered, he walks through the door. Him. Blake.

My face lights up. He got my note. But how did he find

me here? Because he knows. That's why. He can feel me. He can find me anywhere.

I look up, right into his eyes, but he turns away. Doesn't he see me?

Then another boy comes in. I recognize him from the frat party, but don't remember his name. He's tall too, not as tall as Blake, but tall. He's tan with blond hair and blue eyes and a plaid shirt and tweed shorts. Greg? Damon? Charles? Yes, that's it. Charles.

"Hey dude," Charles says.

"Hey," Blake says.

"Over there okay?" Charles asks. He's pointing to the table right next to mine.

Blake nods and they sit down. My skin goes all static electricity like it's been rubbed by a balloon for hours, just waiting for me to touch something and transfer the spark.

Him sitting here? It's a message. A secret message just for me. He must have liked the note. He must have loved it. Now he wants to play a little game with me. Tease me until it's time.

I love games. I love surprises. Of course he'd know that. Of course he would.

They order, make small talk. I listen to everything, no longer caring about my homework.

"Last year, man. Can you fucking believe that shit?" Charles says.

"I know. Time to get serious," Blake says.

"What's that mean? The way I figure, it means we've got

a year to stuff as much party in as possible."

"For you, maybe."

"You're not going to party this year?"

"I didn't say that. I just said it's time to get serious."

"Like how?"

"I figure it's better to find someone this year before things change, you know? I'd rather get somebody loyal, somebody I can trust. Besides, the pool only gets smaller from here."

"Smart, I guess. But geez. Ole' Sick Dick settling down, huh?"

"Yup."

"That's fuckin' crazy."

"Not that crazy. Most people get married after college, don't they?"

"I don't fuckin' know."

"Whatever. Just wait. Two years from now you're gonna have, like, twelve kids snotting up your game."

"Not me, man. No way." The waitress skates up to them with two big plates of burgers and fries. Charles takes a big bite of his burger.

"So who's the lucky girl?"

"No idea yet."

"Got anybody in mind?"

"Maybe. We'll see. I met somebody at the party the other night. This cute freshman. Super hot. Fantastic ass. You wouldn't believe this ass. And smart too. Classy. Pledging Kappa."

"Kappas are really your only option if you're serious about this."

"Exactly. I won't say I'm decided, but she's worth further investigation."

"Ha. I bet. Well, good luck man. I can't even think about that shit right now. I can't imagine getting married until, God, I don't know. Maybe ever."

"Everybody's got to grow up sometime."

They dig into their burgers and the conversation dies down between them.

I can't believe it. I knew we were soul mates, but he wants to get married? It's more than I've ever dreamed of. Fast, yes. But when you know, you know.

As nonchalantly as I can, I stand up. I stare right at Blake as I approach, willing him to look up at me. He does. He looks right into my eyes, holds my gaze, and smiles. There's danger in that smile. A razor's edge of a challenge. Can I handle this? Can I handle him? I can.

I can play games too.

I let my hand reach out, let my fingers brush against his face as I pass. I'll just give him a smidgeon of me. Just a taste. Then I walk right by, letting him have a fantastic view of my fantastic ass as I head toward the restroom. I'd be lying if I said it wasn't an invitation.

I wait in the restroom, wait for him to follow me there, claim me as his own. But he doesn't come.

Eventually, I venture out again. They're gone. He's teaching me a lesson, I decide. A lesson about wanting.

Now I only want him more.

At their table sits a bill and a pile of cash. I don't take much, just a penny, but it's his. His penny. I'll keep it forever.

15

THE FIRST TWO WEEKS OF class go by like a speeding train.

All the magazines say you should play hard to get, but they don't say how hard it is to do. I have to force myself not to call him, not to find out what classes he's taking, not to show up at his door. But I have to be strong. I won't make the same mistake I made with Johnny.

Classes help. Amber and I have Biology together. She's a Finance major and I'm a Mathematics major, so our core requirements are pretty much the same. Still, neither of us knows of anyone else on our floor who is in any of our classes, so it's a happy coincidence. We partner up for lab work to make things easier.

The classes are so different from high school. Instead of giving us a day for orientation, the professors jump right in. Before we know it, we have reading and labs and papers and so much homework I'm not sure how we'll get through it all. Amber sets up a schedule for us to study together during the week so we'll have more time to party on the weekends. Almost no one has classes on Fridays so it's wide open for parties on Thursday night and sleeping in and doing the same thing again every night until Monday morning rolls around again.

"Work hard, play harder. That's what I say," she says.

And she's right. We work hard. Really hard. By the time Friday comes I'm not sure I have any energy left to party with. But Friday is the day we've been looking forward to all week so I have to rally. It's the official beginning of Rush Week.

I had almost forgotten about the Kappas until Blake mentioned it. But now that he has, I have to pledge there. Have to. Kappas are the only true candidates for marriage material. It was a message. He wants me to be a Kappa so I will be a Kappa.

Amber and I dress for orientation night like we're meeting diplomatic ambassadors or something. Every item of clothing is carefully considered. Every accessory selected and discarded and finally settled on as though our lives depend on it. Even the way we do our hair is important.

"They say it doesn't matter what you look like, but they have to say that. Trust me. It matters," Amber says. "Those girls are fricken' judgey."

In the end, we decide on classy casual. I wear a pair of jeans, a flowy cream-colored top, and a rose-colored blazer that sets off my hair, which hangs in loose curls down my back. Amber wears jeans and an electric green blouse with something she calls a statement necklace. It's as green as Blake's eyes but not even close to as sparkly.

Together, we go into the Ford Ballroom. There are so many girls inside it takes my breath away.

"Can you believe this? There have to be at least a thousand girls in here," Amber says.

"I can't believe it," I say. And I can't. I had no idea so many people wanted to be in sororities.

"My heart's goin' all crazy. You do realize there are eleven houses on campus, right? And each of them has maybe two hundred girls at max, which means they're not taking more than fifty each. Which means at least half of us are gonna get cut. What is my momma gonna say if I get cut?"

"We're not getting cut," I say.

"You promise?"

"I promise. It's our destiny."

She rolls her eyes at me and laughs. "You're such a cornball sometimes."

We sign in and then the worst thing happens. We get split up. Right away. Just like that.

They split us into groups, the girls we'll be with throughout the entire Rush process. And Amber and I aren't in the same group.

"There's been a mistake," I say to the girl checking us in. "We wanted to stay together."

"Oh, sorry, we can't do that. We really want you to make a decision about your sorority on your own, so we try to assign the groups randomly," she says. "It's actually better for you if you don't know anybody."

"So there's no way we can do it together?" Amber asks.

"No, I'm sorry."

The look on my face must show her I don't like this little detail. Not one bit.

"Don't worry," the girl at the check-in table says. "It's a great opportunity to meet new people! Which is exactly what Greek life is all about. You'll both have a blast, I swear."

Amber turns to me. "Well, good luck I guess. You're gonna do great."

16

AMBER HUGS ME AND WALKS away. My heart races too now. With her by my side, I felt stronger, better. But now? Now I'm a little fish in a very, very big pond. And I have no idea how to swim.

I make my way toward my rush group. A girl greets me right away. She's gorgeous, with rich, cinnamon skin and long shiny hair that cascades in a glossy sheet from her scalp. About ten other girls who all look so perfect they could be walking down the streets of Hollywood surround her.

"Are you Greta?" she says with a smile. "We're looking for a Greta."

"That's me."

"Welcome to Rush! I'm your Rho Chi. My name is Jessica James. Have a seat."

I take a seat next to the other girls.

"Now that you're all here, let me give you a little overview of how this all works. First of all, I'm here to help you through this process in any way I can. Rush can be pretty overwhelming, and that's why I'm here. If you need outfit advice or have questions, you can call me anytime. Literally any time. If you're sitting in your room, freaking out at three in the morning, I'm the one you call, okay? I mean it."

We all nod. The other girls are smiling big, fake smiles so I paste one on my face too.

"Good. Now the only thing I can't help you with is making a the actual decision of which sorority to choose. I'm in a sorority too, and I, of course, think it's the very best one. So it wouldn't be fair for me to try to sway you one way or the other."

A brunette shoots her hand up. "Which sorority are you in?"

"I'm sorry, but I can't tell you that either. It's a total secret. And for the next week, I can't talk to any of my sisters either. Which sucks for me, I promise, because they're awesome! You might love me, you might hate me, but that shouldn't influence your decision about which sorority you choose at all. And I might love you or hate you too, but since I'm your advisor, my opinion of you shouldn't matter to my sorority either. Does that make sense?"

"Sure," the brunette says. "But do we ever find out?"

"I'll tell you which sorority I belong to on bid day. Who knows? We may end up being sisters. We may not. But I promise you, all the sororities are amazing. Like, so amazing. The Panhellenic Council here is as old as dirt, so they've had a lot of time to work out the kinks."

The other girls nod. I nod too.

"Okay. So why don't we start out by introducing ourselves? I want those conversation skills to shine, ladies! Tell me your name and something about you that we might not know by looking at you. Laney, why don't you start?" Jessica looks to the brunette who asked her the question.

"Hey there, I'm Laney Miles and you wouldn't know it by looking at me, but I'm ambidextrous. I can write with both hands."

"That's crazy!" Jessica says. "Do you just switch back and forth or what?"

"Pretty much, yeah. I grew up watching everyone else write with their right hands, so I tend to lean that way too, but I can do both."

"All right. So cool. Laney is ambidextrous." Jessica turns to me. "How about you, Greta?"

"No."

"Hmm?" Jessica says, confusion twisting her face to a pucker.

"No. I'm not ambidextrous. I'm left-handed." Some of the girls titter behind their hands.

"Oh!" Jessica says. She seems surprised by something. She has a look on her face that seems like she can't believe what I just said. "I meant it's your turn. To tell us something about yourself?"

"Oh, sorry. Okay, umm—"

"Zap!" Jessica says, poking me in the arm.

I stop and stare at her. What was that for?

"Anybody want to take a guess at why Greta got zapped?"

No one says anything.

"'Um' is a no-no word," Jessica says. "It makes you sound insecure, unsure of yourself and what you have to say. The sororities are looking for strong women who know themselves and can speak clearly about their opinions. So I don't want to hear any ums or hmms or anything like that, okay? If you do, I'm gonna zap you!"

"Okay, well, ah—" I say.

"Zap!" Jessica pokes me again. Her nail is sharp, even through my blazer. I recoil away from her and the other girls laugh. My rage is boiling.

How dare she?

"Careful, lady," Jessica says. "That's a bad habit. You really gotta pay attention to it. Right now it doesn't matter. But out there? Those girls notice. Consider this good practice."

I want to poke her back, right in the eye, so hard it pops out into my palm. I glare at her so hard my own eyes might pop out.

"I'm not picking on you, I swear," she says with a smile. "Go on. Give it another try. You got this."

I take a deep breath, clear my head, and make an effort to speak slowly. "My name is Greta Bell," I say. "And you might not know it by looking at me, but I have a 4.0 GPA, or—" I stop myself from saying 'ah,' "I did in high school."

"Much better," Jessica says. "You really nailed it that time. Way to go, Greta. A smart girl like you should be able to catch on fast."

I notice a couple of the other girls roll their eyes and smirk. When we take a break, everyone groups up into little cliques, but no one talks to me.

Later on, we go into the auditorium and they explain about sorority dues ($750 every semester), GPA requirements (3.0 for most houses), and the time commitment being involved in a sorority entails (a lot, apparently.) Then each sorority president gives a short speech about her house, and we're released for the night with instructions to show up early the next morning and report to our Rho Chi.

I find Amber right away. She's talking animatedly to some other girls in her rush group.

"Hey," I say. "Ready to head back?"

"Actually," Amber says. "I was gonna get a bite to eat with my new friends here. Wanna come?"

They're all looking at me like they don't really want me along. All of them except Amber, of course.

"Maybe another time," I say. "I need to get some sleep."

"Okay, sugar. See you later," Amber says, then turns back to her group and is immediately swallowed up into whatever conversation they were having before.

17

TODAY IS OPEN HOUSE DAY. We'll be going from house to house with our rush groups, meeting all the sororities and getting a tour of their houses.

Amber came in late last night, so late I'm surprised she's even standing upright as we get ready for the day.

"What did you do last night?" I ask.

"Oh, nothing. You know," she says and yawns. "Just got some ice cream and talked and stuff. Nothing much. They're really great girls, though. How are the girls in your rush group?"

"Not like that," I say.

"Really? Oh no! That's too bad. But it actually could be good for you. If they're all duds, you'll stand out big time."

I hadn't thought about it like that, but she's right. I smile at her. This is what having a best friend is for.

"What do you think about this outfit?" I ask. We've been told to wear casual attire, so I'm wearing a pair of jeans and a plain white T-shirt.

"Hmm. Needs a little something." She rummages through her closet. "How about this vest? Oh! And I have the perfect necklace."

She hands me the vest. It's dusty blue and made out of T-shirt material that's soft and stretchy and drapes over my butt and hips to hide them. The effect is perfect. I immediately look skinnier.

Then she shows me the necklace, and it's so pretty my breath catches in my throat.

"I know. It's a Rue Michelle. My granny got it for me for Christmas. Don't even ask how much this one cost."

She drapes it around my neck. It's simple—a long gold chain with a blue, blown-glass bauble about the size of a golf ball dangling underneath it. I lift it up to take a closer look and it's like staring into a crystal ball. The shape is so unique, so elegant, that it immediately raises my outfit to the next level.

"I love Rue Michelle. The designer is from London and each piece is handmade, so every one is totally unique and irreplaceable. If you break it, I'll kill you."

"I'll be very careful. I promise," I say, fingering the shiny object dangling from my neck.

"Don't worry about it. Of course you will." Amber stands back to look at me. "Much better. You're gonna kill it."

We walk to the Ford Ballroom to meet our groups. At the door, Amber hugs me goodbye and goes to find her rush group.

I watch her as she prances away, watch as the other girls light up to see her, like the sun just came out and its name is Amber. They lean in to talk to her. They smile and laugh and get so excited. It's a reaction I've never gotten from anyone in my life, but it's instantaneous with her. Something about Amber is pure magic. I wish I could borrow a little of it today.

I pull my gaze away and find my group. No one says hello, but it doesn't matter. Amber is right. It'll make it easier for me to be surrounded by such dull people. I'll shine like a star.

Soon we're off to our first house, the Tri-Alphas. It looks like it could be on a southern plantation: white clapboard and wraparound porch and tons of windows with gauzy white curtains. Jessica has us stand on the lawn, and before we know what's happening, the Alpha girls pour out of the front door and line up like cheerleaders in front of us. They're wearing matching outfits: white shorts and pink T-shirts with three Greek A's across the chest.

Then, no joke, they start singing to the tune of Katy Perry's "California Girls":

Alpha Alpha girls are so incredible!
Three big A's, you know we're on top!
Wisdom, Grace, Poise, and lots of Charity,
That's our priority! Whoa-oh-oh-oh-oh!

They do the entire song with custom lyrics like that. The whole thing is choreographed with hand motions and everything. And loud. I don't know what they do to get so loud, but I have to keep myself from shoving my fingers in my ears.

At the end, they cheer and whoop and jump around. It's infectious. I'm smiling from ear to ear and so is the rest of my rush group. The sorority president comes forward.

"Welcome to Alpha Alpha Alpha! We're so happy to have you here! We'd like to introduce you to our house today. Let's get things started with Amy."

Amy steps forward from the crowd of pink shirts. "Laney Anderson, please enter the house." Amy holds out her hand.

Laney, from my group, looks around. We're not the only group standing on the lawn—there are at least a hundred pledges—all of us a little confused by Laney being singled out. But Jessica nods to her with a smile and she steps forward to take Amy's hand. They go inside.

Another girl steps forward and holds out her hand. "Greta Bell, please enter the house."

I step forward and she grabs my hand and pulls me inside.

"Welcome to the Tri-Alphas," she says. "My name is Casey."

"Hi," I say.

Casey leads me into a large room that looks like it's their living room, only bigger than any living room I've ever seen. Laney is in there too, and soon all the girls in my rush group are led in, followed by all the other pledges from all the other rush groups. Later, Jessica explains you can't enter the houses without a direct invitation from a sister. It's one of the many, many rules.

"So, Greta, tell me a little bit about yourself," Casey says.

"There's not much to tell," I say. Am I supposed to have prepared something? Am I supposed to say the 'what you might not know by looking at me' thing Jessica had us do?

"Well, why don't you tell me why you decided to rush?"

"Um—"

Zap!

"I, ah—"

Zap!

"Hmm …"

Zap!

"Take your time. Trust me, I know this process can be overwhelming, but there's really no pressure."

"What was the question again?"

The girl looks at me with a smile, but the smile seems like it's being pushed out from behind a curtain of patience.

"Why did you decide to rush?"

"Oh, right. I, ah—I decided to rush because my roommate is doing it. Her mom's a Kappa."

"Interesting. But you don't have any special reason why you wanted to rush?"

"Well, to be a Kappa with Amber for one. We're best friends. And, there's this guy, my boyfriend. He really wants me to be a Kappa too."

She raises her eyebrows up and says nothing. Her

expression has gone a little solid.

"Did I say something wrong? I can say something else if you want."

"No. That's okay. I appreciate your honesty. It sounds like you have your heart set on another house. And the Tri-Alphas are really looking for girls who want to be here, not somewhere else. I don't think you'd be a good fit for us anyway."

"Why? Did I do something wrong?"

She lets out a little huff of breath, but before she can speak, someone taps her on the shoulder. It's another Tri-Alpha girl. She's smiling brightly, holding out her hand to shake mine.

"My turn! I'm Leslie. And you are?"

"Greta is going to be a Kappa, Leslie," Casey says with a sarcastic singsong to her voice.

"What? You don't even want to learn about how awesome the Tri-Alphas are?"

"Of course I do. I didn't mean—"

"S-N-A-M, babe, *totally* S-N-A-M," Casey says under her breath to Leslie. Then she turns to me. "Good luck in the rush process, Greta."

Casey leaves to talk to someone else.

"What did she say to you? What's S-N-whatever?" I say.

"Nothing. It doesn't matter," Leslie says. She looks a little nervous.

"Tell me," I say, my tone too harsh. I grab her hand in mine. "Please."

Leslie squirms out of my hand and gives me a look like I could be an octopus or something.

"I said it doesn't matter," Leslie says. Her face has gone hard. She's practically sneering at me, practically spitting venom in my eyes. It reminds me of the way *that girl* used to look at me. It's exactly the way *that girl* used to look at me. I want to scratch her eyes out.

"Jesus Christ. Are all of you this bitchy?" I say.

Leslie huffs then leans in toward me and whispers, "S-N-A-M: so not alpha material." She glares at me. "Sorry, I have to go," she says. Then she's gone, whispering into another girl's ear as they stare at me, alone in a room where no one else is alone. Whispering and staring and making faces at each other and laughing.

And then I'm running.

18

I RACE OUT THE FRONT door of the house. Everyone turns to look as my feet fly me away. I think I hear Jessica James say, "Greta? Where are you going?" but I don't stop.

I run and run, down the block and around the corner, putting space between those awful girls and me. My feet rub against shoes meant for standing prim and proper. The shoes are certainly not meant for this—this mad dash away from those eyes. Those looks. The staring and the laughing and the just-like-high-school-ness of it all.

I find a path that winds behind houses, follows a stream. I race along the bank, letting my lungs go tight, letting my muscles burn. Then I round a bend and see where the stream empties into a lake. My body aches from it all and I haven't eaten anything today and everything feels wobbly and wrong. I land on the bank of the lake and stare out toward a flock of ducks, swimming in desperate circles, their heads down searching for food.

I hate them. I hate those girls.

And I'm tired, so tired, of being the girl people laugh at.

College was supposed to be different. College was supposed to be better. For a while, I thought it was. But it was only a lie I told myself. It was a stupid, stupid lie to believe I could ever be anything but Gassy-G. I'll always be a loser.

So what now? What does my future hold now that I know the truth? Should I pack up and go home? Not that my parents would take me. Should I transfer to a different school? Try for a scholarship somewhere else? What's the point? It'll be the same everywhere. No one understands me.

No one except Blake.

That's right. Blake. My Blake. My sun and my stars and my moon and my sky. He loves me. And he is so good, so handsome, so amazing. How could anyone as amazing as Blake love an outcast?

I hiccup the last tears out of my throat as I realize it's not possible. He couldn't love someone who wasn't on his level.

But he does love me, which means I am.

I am on his level.

I am good enough to love.

It's those girls, those bitchy, bitchy girls at Tri-Alpha who are to blame. No wonder Blake didn't say he was interested in marrying anyone but a Kappa. All the other sororities are empty, stupid, ugly whores.

And girls like the ones at Tri-Alpha? Bitchy cunts who don't know a real winner when they see one? They're the worst of the bunch. They're what make this world a bad place. They're the ones who have to pay.

And I know just how I'll make them pay. Exactly how.

I find the restroom inside a Burger King and clean myself up, then get a value meal to keep myself from passing out. Tonight, the Tri-Alphas will pay for what they did to me. But today? Today I have to make sure I'm still in the running to be a Kappa.

After I eat, I go to the Kappa house and wait in the street. According to the schedule in my purse, my rush group should arrive soon. After a couple minutes, I see them walking down the street, laughing and lively, excited to be courted by the next house. Jessica spots me and bounds toward me.

"Greta? Where have you been? We've been so worried about you."

But from the looks on the other girls' faces, it's clear Jessica is the only one who was worried. The others look like they barely remember I was there.

"I'm sorry, I didn't feel well," I say. "I didn't want to make a spectacle of myself so I stepped away for a moment. But I feel much better now."

"Oh, that's really too bad. You've missed almost all the house tours, and there really isn't a way to go back to visit them. I'm so sorry."

"It's okay. I already know which house I want. I want to be a Kappa."

She turns her head, raises her eyebrows like she's surprised.

"Well, then I guess you're in luck."

Just as she says it, the Kappas come out of the house, all two hundred of them, white-toothed and shiny-haired and dressed in white, eyelet summer dresses that sway in the breeze. They are perfect. I can see right away what Blake sees in the Kappas, what everyone must see. They're not dressed in slutty shorts and sloppy T-shirts like the Tri-Alphas. They look like models. They look like CEOs. They look like the embodiment of all that is good and wholesome and honorable in the world.

I don't regret missing any of the other houses. I'm where I'm supposed to be. I'm a Kappa.

Their music starts. It's not brassy and childish like the Tri-Alphas. They're so much more than that, so much better. This is a song I've never heard before. I think as I listen to it that the song must have been written just for them, maybe even *by* them.

Oh, the Kappas heart-light shines!
On sisterhood in the dark times.
On faces true and faces bold.
We are Kappas, young and old.

Oh, Kappa, my Kappa,
My sisters tried and true.
Oh Kappa, my Kappa,

I am your sister too.

Oh, the colors gold and white!
Light our way through the black night.
With truth, elegance, virtue,
The Kappa shines in all you do.

Oh, Kappa, my Kappa,
My sisters tried and true.
Oh Kappa, my Kappa,
I am your sister too.

Oh, the dahlia flower fine!
May our beauty be divine
Oh, the sun with bright gold rays!
May clear vision light our way.

Oh, Kappa, my Kappa,
My sisters tried and true.
Oh Kappa, my Kappa,
I am your sister too.

Their voices soar, sweet and loud and mingling with a soft breeze that floats up to the heavens. I love it. I love every word and nuance and tone.

These girls don't need stupid cheerleader-esque choreography. They stand perfectly still and command everyone's absolute attention. That's what true class is about. That's what true poise looks like. The Tri-Alphas could learn some lessons watching them.

Oh, Kappa, my Kappa,
My sisters tried and true.
Oh Kappa, my Kappa,
I am your sister too.

We are all breathless as they finish.

Then a girl steps forward, and they begin calling names from my group. They go in reverse alphabetical order until there are only two of us left. Laney and Me.

A petite brunette steps forward, her skin sun-kissed and her hair flecked with strands of auburn. She holds her hand out to me, and I know right away we will be fast friends.

"Greta Bell, would you please enter the house?" she says.

I take her hand and squeeze it, just a little squeeze. She turns to me and smiles as we walk into one of the most beautiful foyers I've ever seen.

Two mahogany staircases twist from the entry up into a broad landing above. In the center, there's a crystal chandelier that sparkles sunbeams across the space. It's breathtaking.

The girl leads me to a sitting room on the right. Like the Tri-Alpha house, it is expansive enough to be a small ballroom. Unlike the Tri-Alpha house, it is immaculate: wingback chairs and tufted settees, Tiffany lamps and mirrored hutches. All of the decor is in the house colors of gold and white.

The girl who brought me in sits on one of the settees and motions for me to join her. Her back is straight, her ankles crossed, her hands folded in her lap. I mimic her pose, down to the fingers, down to the vertebrae stacked one on top of the other to make my spine upright and regal.

"I'm Claire," she says. "It's a pleasure to meet you."

"No, it's my pleasure," I say with a smile like we're both inside a movie from the 1950's. It feels like we are. Something like *Serena* or *When the Bell Tolls*, back in the days when people were civilized.

"I have to ask. Is that a Rue Michelle necklace?"

I finger the bauble on my neck. I had almost forgotten it was there at all. "It is. One of a kind. Handmade," I say.

"I just love Rue Michelle," Claire gushes. "It's my absolute favorite designer. I have three of their pieces, but if I had my way it would be a hundred."

"I know!" I say. "Me too! I'm starting a campaign now to get my grandma to buy me another one for Christmas."

"That's a good idea. I love a girl who plans ahead," she says.

"If I'm anything, I'm a planner," I say, even though it's not really true. But it could be. I can change.

"Well then, we should get along just fine," Claire says. "So tell me, Greta, why did you decide to participate in rush this semester?"

"Because I want to be a Kappa," I say confidently. "I've done my research and I know it's the house for me."

Claire's grin goes all wide. "I think I might have just found my rush crush."

19

LATER THAT NIGHT AMBER AND I are back in our dorm room, sitting at the computer, logged into the program that tallies the matches between sorority houses and PNMs—potential new members. Tonight, we've been instructed to drop the list down from the eleven sororities on campus to the seven sororities we'd like to continue to pursue. Back at the houses, the sororities are doing the same thing with us, culling the list of girls. Tomorrow the computer will tell us which sororities on our list also want to see us.

"Ugh. I don't know what to do," Amber says. "Kappa stays on the list, obviously. But there's also the Delta Gamma Nus and the Omega Tau Iotas. They were all so nice, I can't decide who to drop."

"Did you really think so?" I say.

"Which ones are you dropping?"

"The Tri-Alphas for sure. Those girls were really tacky."

"You think? They seemed nice to me."

"No. Definitely not. I'm cutting them. And, God, I don't really know who else. But I honestly don't care either. I've already decided I want to be a Kappa."

"But what if they don't pick you? Don't you want a backup?"

"Why would I want a backup? If the Kappas don't pick me, I don't want to be in a sorority at all."

Amber looks at me, a little taken aback. I can tell this surprises her. A week ago I didn't even know what a Kappa was.

"You're so much bolder than I am, Greta. I really admire that." She turns back to the computer. "You know what? Screw it. The Tri-Alphas are out and so is Theta Rho Phi."

She taps a few keys on the computer and is finished. Then I do mine.

"I feel much better now," Amber says. "Want to get some ice cream at Stanton's?"

"Actually, I have something I have to do tonight," I say.

"What?"

"Just an assignment for English Composition. I'm supposed to write a poem about nature or something, so I thought I'd take a walk for inspiration."

"Oh, cool. I'll go with you."

"Actually, I think I better go alone."

Her face falls a little, and it kills me to hurt her like this. But what I'm doing? She can't be there.

Then her face lights up, grinning and knowing. "You don't have to write about nature at all. We have the same professor for English Comp. We have an assignment on persuasive writing, which I know for a fact you've already done."

I freeze. It has to happen tonight. It has to. Or they won't know. They'll think they got away with it.

"I, ah—it's not—"

Amber sidles up to me with a grin. "You're going to meet that boy, aren't' you?"

Relief washes over me. "Busted," I say.

"You fussy little hussy, you," she says. "You're a secretive thing, aren't you?"

"I guess I'm just private."

"Okay, go. By all means don't let me be the one to get in the way of a little yum-yum."

This makes me laugh. "Yum-yum? What is yum-yum?"

"You know … *it*," she says. "Doin' it."

"You call making love 'yum-yum'?"

"Ewe! You call it making love? That's way grosser."

"It's better than yum-yum." I laugh.

"Shut your mouth and get out of here."

"I am," I say.

"Quick. Before I have to think about you *making love*. Ulgh. That's so disgusting."

I grab my backpack and go. "Whatever. See you later."

The conversation with Amber makes me feel so much better about the day. So much better I almost consider not carrying out my plan for tonight. Almost.

It's easy enough to find the house again. It sits mostly quiet, a lone light on in the front room where the girls are likely casting votes for who's moving on to the next round and who's getting dropped tomorrow. I can see the darkness of all the other windows, can watch the shadows passing along the curtains, can hear the murmur of a heated discussion leaking through the walls.

My timing couldn't be more perfect.

I walk right up onto the porch, its wood creaking and dry, in need of a paint job to cover its age. No one hears me.

It's easy enough to sneak in through their back gate. It's not locked. There's no guard dog, no one around at all.

I light the match in the back of the house, where I can see the kitchen through the windows. I can see the appliances too: the toaster oven, the gas stove. I imagine them bursting. I imagine the heat in the room consuming the rest of the house. I imagine the screams of the girls inside, imagine Casey's shriek, imagine Leslie's tears.

I hold up the match to the old wood and the flames lick at the slats like a lover, wanting and passionate. By the time I step back, a spike of orange three feet tall dances against the wall.

I smile.

I go.

20

THE NEXT MORNING I GET some news I expected and some news I didn't.

The Ford Ballroom is full again for stage two of recruitment, but they won't give us our visit lists yet. They make us all find our rush groups and sit down, with warnings to be quiet and respectful.

Tearfully, the Tri-Alpha president gets on stage and explains that they had a tragic fire. Apparently they think it started somewhere in the kitchen, but the fire chief is looking into it. The fire was so bad it claimed half their house and sent two sisters to the hospital for smoke inhalation. And because of it all, their recruitment efforts this semester must cease. Sadly, they won't be taking on any new members.

This surprises me, but only because she's standing on stage at all. And only half the house? I had hoped the damage would be much worse than that.

There's a collective shock and awe and worry that passes

through the room when she finishes speaking. Tears too. Some girls break down, crying that they wanted to pledge Tri-Alpha, that it's not fair. I sit quietly, glad the Tri-Alphas won't, at the very least, be able to add to their ranks until the Spring.

Finally, the Rho Chi's pass out our visitation lists. This is the list of sororities who want to see more of us and a schedule of when the visits will occur. While we're still technically a part of a rush group, we won't be spending any more time with them unless our visits coincide. It's a relief to know I won't have to deal with those other girls anymore after today.

When Jessica hands me my list, I get the news I expected. Every house has dropped me from the next stage of recruitment except the Kappas.

It's a good sign, I decide. An excellent sign.

Jessica gives me a little hug. "It's okay, Greta. You've learned a lot this semester, right? And you got so sick yesterday it's really a shame no one else got to meet you. Even if you don't get a bid from the Kappas, you shouldn't worry. There's always next semester, right?"

"I'm not worried. I'm going to be a Kappa," I say.

"Oh, I didn't mean they weren't going to pick you," Jessica says. "I only meant—"

"I know what you meant," I say. "But I'm not worried. I *will* be a Kappa."

She just raises her eyebrows and nods. "Well, good luck to you then."

I leave her and go find Amber to see how she made out. And, of course, every single sorority, every single one, wants to see her again. Even the ones she dropped. It shows on the form even though it doesn't show up on the schedule.

"It's so annoying," she says. "I can't possibly be a good match for all of them. Now my day's gonna be hectic as all get out. How'd you do?"

"The Kappas want to see me again," I say.

"That's awesome!" she says. "What time is your visit?"

"Twelve-thirty," I say.

"Me too!" she says. "I'll see you there!"

With Amber by my side, the next days go by in a cotton candy whirl. It's like riding a carousel, all pomp and pageantry, and all to convince us we should be Kappas. Ever since hearing that Blake wants me to be a Kappa, I've thought about it this way—that they have to convince *me*. It's given me exactly the confidence I need to get through this.

We watch skits and sing songs and bake cookies to sell at a charity bake sale for the Kappa's primary philanthropy group—the Children's Hunger Project. There are special dances to learn and so many names to remember. But since I only have one sorority to focus on, I remember everything.

At one point, the Kappas even close a circle around us and do a special chant. It is magic and midnight and I can't wait to be one of them next year, chanting around PNMs. Amber tells me later there are lots of special chants like this.

Sacred songs and secret handshakes and passwords too. It's all so secret even her mom won't tell her any of it unless she officially joins the sorority. I love secrets. I love the ritual of the whole thing.

It takes all my focus to be as bright and engaging as Amber is. Every last bit. But I do it. Every morning that week, there's a visitation list waiting for me with the Kappa sorority listed on it.

Every day gets dressier and dressier too. We start out casual, then move up to summer dresses, then skirts and heels, until, finally, it's Thursday night, Pref Night, formal cocktail attire. Tonight, everyone has narrowed their selection list down to only two sororities they're thinking of choosing. There is a final party to attend for each house where it's the very last chance to impress the sisters. Tomorrow, they will choose.

I, of course, am only going to the Kappa party, but Amber has two sororities left on her list: the Kappas and Delta Gamma Nu. There are two party times listed for her, and her Kappa party time is different than my own.

It makes me nervous to be there without her, but I try not to worry about it. I am a Kappa. I am I am I am.

I wear the red dress I wore the night I met Blake. It's good luck. Amber helps me pile my hair on my head and lends me a pair of diamond studs, real diamonds, to set off the whole look. When I glance in the mirror, I've never felt more stunning. Never in my life.

Amber looks amazing too in pearls and an LBD (little

black dress, she said) that she bought specifically for tonight.

She grips my hands in hers. "You're gonna do great," she says.

"You're shaking," I say.

"I know. I'm so nervous I almost feel like the butterflies in my stomach are gonna fly outta' my mouth."

"Don't be silly. The Kappas are gonna love you."

"You think?" she says.

"I *know*. By this time tomorrow, we're going to be sisters."

"God, I hope you're right."

We cheek-kiss each other as we part ways. Then Amber heads to Delta Nu and I head to the Kappa house.

It's beautiful outside the house at night. White lights twinkle in the trees and make the ivy on the house send dusty shadows against the bricks. I feel a swell in my chest as Claire, the girl who invited me in the first time I was at the Kappa house, steps outside and calls my name.

"Greta Bell, would you please enter the house?"

She's smiling wide and her eyes are shining just like mine. We've been getting along so well since that first day. I can tell we're going to be lifelong friends.

Inside, everything is candlelit and perfect. Soft music plays. Other girls, much fewer tonight than any other event, mingle in tight, chatty circles. I wonder which of them will be my sisters too?

"You look amazing, honey. That dress is to die for." Claire says.

"Thanks. It's my lucky dress," I say.

"Lucky dress? Why is that?"

"Because I met the love of my life when I wore it the first time."

"The love of your life? Now that sounds juicy. You have to tell me all about it. Who is he? Does he go to Culford?"

"He does," I say, with a shy little grin. I'm not sure I should be telling anyone about us yet, even though I want to, so bad. I want to tell the whole world.

"Who is he? Do I know him? What's his name?"

"I … I don't know if I should say anything. It's really new."

"Don't get coy on my now, sweetie. Tell. I swear I won't say a word to anyone." Her face is gleeful, excited. And we are about to be sisters, aren't we?

"His name is Blake. Blake Abbott."

A cloud passes across her face. "Blake Abbott? The SigUp president?"

"You know him?"

"I, uh, I do," Claire says. "Oh, honey. I don't quite know what to say."

"What?" I ask.

She reaches out to touch my arm. "He's not really … I don't know. I can't, in good faith, recommend you date him."

"Why not?" I can feel the fire licking my heart, but I try to keep it in check. There has to be some misunderstanding.

"It means … there are a lot of girls who fall for Blake. And trust me. I understand the draw. But they never …

they're never happy afterward."

"What is that supposed to mean?" The fire in my chest kicks up into my throat. I feel hot, sticky, agitated like a cobra ready to strike.

She takes a deep breath, looks around the room to make sure no one else is listening. "It means I know from personal experience, okay? It would be better if you stopped seeing him."

I understand perfectly now.

"You know, Claire, I really thought we were going to be good friends. I really did."

"Greta, I—"

"But this jealousy? I expect more out of a sister."

"It's not jealousy, Greta. Not even close. Just trust me, okay? He doesn't deserve you."

The fire goes hot, full blast, like an explosion up from my gut, so tall it's flashing behind my eyes. How dare she? How dare she?

"You lying little whore," I say, standing up until I tower over her, until she's small, sniveling beneath me.

"That's totally unfair. You really don't know what you're talking about."

"I don't know what I'm talking about? Me? Maybe you should take a look in the mirror."

"Greta—"

"No. Stop talking. You don't get to talk to anymore. Not about me and definitely not about Blake. I mean, seriously? Trying to tell me he's some kind of Lothario, just so you can get another shot at him? That's disgusting. You should be ashamed of yourself. Blake is an amazing man. You're lucky you ever got to stand in the same room as him."

"What's going on over here?" Alexis, the chapter president, says. It's not until I hear her that I realize the room has gone totally quiet and everyone is staring.

"Claire is spreading lies," I say. "You need to get your sister in check."

"Excuse me?" Alexis says.

"I said you need to do something about her. Do you really want your organization to be represented that way?"

"I think you should leave," Alexis says.

"But it wasn't my fault. She's the one telling lies."

Alexis leans in close so no one else can hear her. "Claire has been my sister for three years. In all that time, I've never heard her tell a single lie. Not one. I trust her with my life. Which is, by the way, the only reason you're standing in this room at all. Everyone else had doubts about you. Like, every single other person in the house. But she said you had potential. She said to give you a chance. So we did. But now? Now you need to go before I call the cops to escort you out."

21

I WALK HOME, EVERY TREACHEROUS step in high heels that pinch at my toes every time they touch down. It's not fair. It's totally not fair. She was making Blake sound like such a bad person. I had to defend him. I had to.

Now everything is ruined. All I want to do is see Blake, have him hold me in his strong arms and tell me everything will be okay.

I decide to find him, to tell him about what happened tonight. He should know. Besides, the Kappas and SigUp are sibling organizations. And he's the president. If anyone can do something about this, it's him.

But when I knock on the SigUp door, no one answers. It's completely dark inside. I decide to leave him a note instead.

Dearest Darling,

You wouldn't believe what's happened tonight. A girl in the Kappa house, Claire Emory, is telling outright lies about you. But when I tried to defend you (and I was the only one, darling), they kicked me out.

Is there anything you can do? I know how badly you want me to be a Kappa, so please speak to them. It would be a disgrace if I didn't get a bid because of someone else's lies.

All my love, all my heart, all my everything,

Your Darling

I make it home and collapse into my bed and cry and cry until I fall asleep.

I wake up to the sound of Amber coming into our room. Her face is all dreamy-excitement and puppy-dog tails.

"Can you believe this night? I mean, can you even believe it?" she says.

"No. I can't."

"How did it go at the Kappa house?"

"I'm not sure," I say, but I am sure. The sleep has done me good. Now I can see more clearly. Blake will fix this. He has to. "Good, I think."

"They were asking me tons of questions about you. How long we'd been friends, how well we knew each other, if I had met your parents. All sorts of stuff."

"Really?"

"Honestly, I was a little worried for a while that they wanted to take you and not me. But I don't know, I definitely left with a really good feeling about it."

"But they were definitely asking you questions about me?" Blake must have talked to them, then. He must have.

"Yeah. I think they must be really interested in you. I couldn't really tell them much, though. I mean, we haven't really known each other that long."

"I know. That's what makes our friendship so amazing."

She looks at me a little funny, then smiles. "Right," she says. "Oh! Did you see some weirdo at your party? No one would tell me anything, but I overheard this girl telling another girl they almost had to call the police on a crazy PNM."

"No way," I say.

"Seriously. Some bitches be cray-cray when it comes to rushing."

"I guess so," I say. Then, to change the subject, "So, have you made your decision?"

She gets a big smile on her face. "Well, I tried to go into the whole rush process with an open mind. I really didn't want my mom's opinion to sway me one way or the other. But, in my heart? I just really fell in love with those girls. I want to be a Kappa. Like, more than anything."

My heart explodes and a giant grin erupts on my face.

"That's great, Amber. That's really great. Tomorrow, we're going to officially be sisters!"

Amber's rush group is sitting right next to mine in the Ford Ballroom, and the energy in here is electric. There are no chairs, just groups of girls sitting in circles and crossing their fingers for luck. And a lot less than before. There are only maybe six hundred of us left. Of the ten girls I started out with, seven remain. None of us has gotten our bid cards yet, but I'm not nervous. I know Blake will take care of things for me.

Up front, there's a dance performance going on. All the Rho Chis are wearing neon green T-shirts and teasing us like they're about to do a striptease—which they sort of are. Underneath the neon green lies another shirt—a shirt showing which sorority they're in. Now that our decisions have been made and our fates have been decided, they can tell us which house they belong to.

Four of the forty or so Rho Chi's—including Jessica, my group leader—dance forward and pull off their T-shirts, revealing bright white shirts with a giant gold K on the front. They're all Kappas!

All the girls in our circle break out into applause, murmuring "that's great" and "aww" and all the stupid niceties people say when they really don't care.

Only I smile and look her in the eye as she dances back to her place in the dance. Only I know that soon we will be sisters. I hadn't thought about her as Kappa material before, but now, I guess I can see it.

After the Kappas reveal themselves, the rest of the Rho Chis do too—each in small groups, one sorority at a time.

When they're done, we all clap wildly and the Rho Chis come back to their groups with stacks of envelopes, one for each girl.

I reach out for mine expectantly, but before Jessica gives them to anyone, she has instructions. "I'm going to give these to you, but that doesn't mean you can open them yet, understand?"

We all nod.

"I want you to put them under your backsides and sit on them until it's time. I know it sounds silly, but it's tradition," she beams. "I did it, and all my sisters before me did it too."

She hands out the envelopes and I almost disobey and open it right there, but the look she gives me makes me stop. I sit on it like everyone else. It's like we're kindergartners playing duck-duck-goose.

The bid envelope feels hot on my bottom: burning through my jeans, branding my skin. I can feel the Kappa gold screaming for me to accept it as my own. Soon. So soon.

A tapping on the microphone interrupts my thoughts.

Some random girls get on stage and talk, for forever, about I don't know what. And I'm guessing no one else does either. All we're thinking about is what's written on our bid cards. I think the speakers are saying something about how great rush week has been and on and on and on.

Finally, the Culford Panhellenic Council President says, "Okay girls, in a very short moment I'm going to let you open those envelopes. If your rush week ends here, let me just take a moment to say that all of us have really enjoyed getting to know each and every one of you. Many, many girls go on to rush in the spring if they aren't selected in the fall, so you shouldn't consider your Greek experience finished by any means.

"But, for those of you who are lucky enough to receive bids, it's going to be a very exciting day. And it all starts with a very special tradition here at Culford. Your houses are waiting out on the front lawn for you right now!"

Just then, the door swing open and there's a roar from outside. Our heads swing back to look. All I can make out is a blur of color, collections of teeming pink or blue or gold or yellow or green, each sorority standing in a group and yelling so loud it's like we're at a football game and just scored a touchdown. Then each sorority raises its letters—giant, hand-painted letters—representing their houses.

A collective cheer erupts from the crowd to match the one outside. Our energy in here is intense and unbridled. We're wild horses penned up and waiting to run.

"So as soon as you find out what sorority you're in, I want you to run outside and find your house and meet your brand new sisters!"

Another huge cheer.

"Okay. Who's ready to read their bids?"

The crowd explodes. We're all clapping and cheering and so ready to start this incredible new part of our lives. I look over at Amber, and she gives me the most desperate look I've ever seen in my life. Then she crosses her fingers and closes her eyes. I feel bad for her. She's not guaranteed a spot like I am. She doesn't have Blake in her corner.

Suddenly, I'm scared for her too. What if she doesn't make it into the Kappas? She'd be absolutely devastated. I don't even want to think about what her mom will say.

"Okay, ladies. On the count of three. One. Two." She waits a forever amount of time, so long there are shouts from the crowd.

"Come on!"

"Please!"

"Three! Open them up!"

Sounds of tearing paper. My hand reaching under me so quick, fumbling for the envelope, screams around me, tears. A slice across my index finger. A thin line of blood.

Then pulling it out, thick card stock with gold lettering. Gold!

Greta Bell:

We regret to inform you that your bid to be a member of the Kappa Kappa Nu sorority has been unsuccessful. Many wonderful girls rushed this year and we simply couldn't take all of them. Best wishes in your college career.

Sincerely,

Alexis Franklin

Kappa Kappa Nu Chapter President

A smear of my blood across the cream paper.

The flutter of the envelope to the floor.

Screaming and cheering and tears all around me. People running, bolting toward the door. Others hugging and crying. But me still, solid, frozen.

Then Amber's face, an explosion of a smile, so wide the sun might have sparked its glow from hers. She's in. She's a Kappa. She made it.

She looks at me. A cloud over the sun. A flash of pity in her eyes. Then her running over and words I can't hear. A quick hug. The smell of her perfume, floral and cloying.

Amber looks at me again, then at the door. She hesitates.

"Sorry," she says. "I'm really sorry!"

Then she runs outside without looking back.

22

I WALK ZOMBIE-SLOW OUT the door.

On the lawn, I watch as Amber is swallowed into the white and gold Kappa crowd. They're clapping, cheering, and chanting a chant that's drowned out in all the other chanting from all the other houses, all the other girls.

I watch them pull a gold and white T-shirt over her head, twist the stem of a dahlia into her hair, hand her a huge tote bag full of who knows what. I watch them do the same to the other girls they picked, none of whom I recognize. I watch as, elbows locked in a tight chain, the Kappas race away, down the street, and toward the Kappa house.

As I walk back to the dorm alone, the idea registers in my chest hard and heavy and cold, like an anvil dropped in the Arctic Ocean: Amber picked them.

The only time I see Amber for the next full week is in Biology. She doesn't sleep in our dorm, she sleeps in the Kappa house, even though she doesn't even have an official room there.

There are notes from her. Little signs she's been there like clothes missing from her closet, her laptop gone, something on her desk moved an inch to the left, but nothing else.

It's quiet in our room. Too quiet. Too silent. Like the air went away.

And every time she sees me in class that week, the conversation goes something like this:

"Ugh. You would hate it. There's so much to do. They have me running around every stinkin' minute. I swear, I almost regret it."

"So quit."

"Do you know what my momma would do if I quit? She'd string me up by my toes is what. She's so excited. Like, literally, off her rocker crazy about it. But seriously, Greta, you're so much better off. I envy you. I really do."

She's playing a game, but this one I don't like. I can see the thrill in her eyes even if she thinks I'm too dumb to notice. Some girls think they're so slick.

In class on Thursday, I think she can see for a moment that I'm not buying it. So she tries to change the subject.

"How's that guy you've been seeing?"

"Okay," I say. It's confusing right now. I don't know what to make of what he did. Or didn't do. Did he even talk to them? Or did they not listen? I don't know what to think right now. Everything feels so upside down.

"Just okay? You seemed really into him."

"I am. It's just been a really busy week is all. You know,

lots of homework. It's hard to have time for romance right now."

"Tell me about it," she says. "Do you remember that guy I hung out with the first night we went out? His name's Blake?"

"Yeah. I remember."

She smiles, leans in to talk to me more privately. "Well, we ran into each other at this Greek mixer thing and he asked me out."

"Excuse me?"

"I know. I was like, dude, I'm sorry, but this sorority thing has me a little crazy right now."

"So you told him no?"

"Well … not exactly. He was really persistent. And really persuasive, too. I'm kind of a sucker for a guy who won't give up. But I did tell him in no uncertain terms that he was going to have to wait until pledge week was over. Because, I mean, come on. Who has time for that, right?"

Later that night, I write Blake another letter.

Dear Blake,

I don't get it. First you refuse to intervene when I put myself on the line for you. Now this? Did you think I wouldn't find out? Did you think I wouldn't know you asked my roommate out on a date? We tell each other everything.

I know you must be upset that I didn't make it into the Kappas, but you have to understand. I was only sticking up for you. I love you with my whole heart. Everything I do, I do for you—to make you happy, to make you strong. Why are you doing this to me?

She has you under her spell, doesn't she? She had me under her spell too, before I saw her true colors. There are some things you should know about Amber. Bad things. She doesn't love you. Not even a little bit. She wants to use you. She just wants to have fun. She's not serious about love. Not like I am. Do you really want to be wasting time on a girl like that?

Every minute you refuse to see the truth is a minute robbed from our loving each other.

Please, I'm begging you. Tell me what I can do to stop this. Tell me what you want from me. I will do anything. Be your slave, be your dog, be the ground you walk on. Just tell me.

My heart, my love, my everything,

Your Darling

Part Five

My Johnny

23

THE BEST THING, I DECIDE, is to write Johnny a letter.

Dear Johnny, my Darling, my ONE and Only Love,

I can't imagine how hurt you must feel by what I did. I need you to know the truck driver meant nothing to me. I didn't even know his name, I swear!

I know a lot of people who say that and don't really mean it. They're just trying to make excuses for what they did to make the other person take them back or make them feel better. But for me it's true. In fact, it's almost the opposite of the truth the way I mean it.

Because I wanted you that night, nobody else.

But you were with that GIRL. That little girl! I don't

understand it. I'm a woman, the woman of your heart. If you look deep inside, you know that's true. Some people (that GIRL) might tell you that you don't care about me. But you and I know the truth. You can feel it. Can't you? Can't you?

I know you can. I can see the way you look at me. You want me as much as I want you.

It's just my foolish weakness that separates us. What I've done has ripped a hole in our connection. I understand that and I'm so sorry. You can't imagine how sorry. If I could take it back, I would. But I can't. You need to see that. You need to forgive me. Just tell me what to do!

Do you want to know what I was thinking about when I was with him?

I was thinking about you. His hands became your hands. His mouth became your mouth. I closed my eyes and I saw your face. It was you I was kissing the whole time. Don't you understand that?

You and I are supposed to be together. It's our destiny.

Can't you feel the tug your heart makes when I'm around? Can't you see my love for you in everything I do? It's all for you, my love. I go to class only because I know you're in the same building. I do my homework only because it makes me better, smarter, for you. I wash the dishes hoping one day I'll be standing at our sink, in our house. I'll feel your arms circle around my waist. I'll splash water at you for fun and you will kiss me with a love deeper than anything anyone has ever felt.

Our life together is just a whisper away. All you need to do is forgive me. Please end the torture I feel in my heart.

All my love,

Greta

P.S. I'm trying to be understanding about THAT GIRL, *but it is hard.*

24

I THINK IT'S WORKING, SO I keep writing. Whenever I think of him, I write—which ends up being a lot.

My Darling,

Do you want to know what I was thinking about today in Biology? I was thinking of how surprised you looked when you opened your locker and saw my last letter. The thought of you being happy makes me so amazingly happy. It makes my heart soar!

I started to dream about our life together. You're so talented! I just know you're going to be a famous director someday. I just know it. Can you imagine all the parties we'll attend? All the glamorous events? Me on your arm at the Academy Awards? I'll be the one crying the hardest when you win your first Oscar. Will you tell our kids to go to bed in your acceptance speech or will you tell them

Daddy loves them? Maybe both! I'll kill the band if they play you off stage, you know I will.

I already know what we're going to wear! It's silly, I know, but don't make fun of me, okay? Because it's actually sweet too. We'll wear the same thing we wore on our Wedding Day. Me in my wedding gown and you in that tux. Can you imagine it? Everyone will be so touched and know how much we love each other.

Please forgive me so we can start making our plans.

Lovingly yours,

Greta

P.S. I bet that GIRL hasn't even heard of the Academy Awards.

25

RELATIONSHIPS ARE HARD. SOMETIMES THINGS come up between Johnny and I that I never expected at all. That's when communication is especially important.

My love,

My love, my love, my darling boy. I am in such distress over us! You wouldn't believe!

Can you imagine how my heart dropped when I watched you kiss HER today? It was a knife to my heart.

I know I deserve it for what I did. I know you're just teaching me a lesson, and as soon as you're ready to forgive me, we'll be together forever and ever and always and forever.

I know you can't really love her, never could LOVE someone like that GIRL, even if she tells you lies to try and get you to love her. But sometimes, like when I saw the way you looked at her this morning, I get scared. She's not convincing you, is she? With her LIES?

Because she is a liar. Just today I saw her looking at Brendan Simms exactly the way she looks at you. She wanted to claim him too!

I don't think you know the danger you're in. That GIRL is a KNOWN TEMPTRESS. She's seduced so many other boys before you and only left a trail of tears behind her. You're strong, I know you are, stronger than anyone I've ever met. And more handsome AND more smart!

So have your fun with her if you must but please don't succumb to her. She will hurt you. That's all she wants to do. I can see it in her eyes. It hurts me to see you suffer, especially when all I want to do is make you happy the way you deserve to be happy.

My love, you're hurting me so much with all of this! Please end my pain.

Please, my darling, my love, my only one. I can't stand this much longer. Forgive me. Please.

All yours and only yours,

Greta

P.S. Enclosed is a hair from "down there." I will pluck one every day for you until you come to me. Every single day. Would that GIRL do the same for you? She wouldn't. She doesn't care.

26

I'VE BEEN SENDING THE LETTERS for a year, but I can tell he's still mad. He doesn't talk to me at all. He doesn't even smile at me in the halls anymore. He spends all his time with *that girl*. And she's even gotten all their friends to start calling me names. "Gassy-G" is their favorite, but there's also "Psycho Bitch" and "Stalk-er-ella."

I deserve it. I know I do. I deserve a lot worse for what I did to him.

Junior year passes, and I spend the entire summer trying to figure out what else I can do, but I can't come up with anything, so I keep on sending the letters.

But eventually, I've had enough of *that girl's* tricks. If Johnny won't do something about her, then I will. If I could just keep her from spending so much time with him, then I know I could get through to him. But she's always near him, always blocking me. It has to stop. It has to stop tonight, at his football game.

She's usually there, cheering him on. But tonight it will

be me. Not her. Me.

I ditch my last class and find her dumb car in the parking lot near the tennis court—the senior lot. It's one of the newer Volkswagen Beetles, painted a sickening mint green. Her parents spoil her. I know she doesn't have a job—otherwise she wouldn't be able to spend every waking moment draining the life out of Johnny.

I pull the knife out of my backpack—the one I got from my dad's workshop. There's no one around right now—everyone's in class—but I still feel nervous doing what I'm about to do.

I jab the knife into her tire, but it doesn't go through. It's harder than I thought. The rubber is thick and my knife is dull. I try again, positioning the knife's tip at a part of the tire that looks thinner and pressing my entire body weight into it.

Soon there is a satisfying hiss, then the blade breaks all the way through, making me lose my balance and fall against the car. As I regain my stance, I watch the tire drain of air until it's completely deflated.

I repeat the process three more times on the other wheels. That should do the trick.

I find a place to hide—behind some bushes that line the tall fence of the tennis court. It's not a perfect view, but it should be close enough to hear.

The final bell rings, and not long after, I hear her voice.

"Oh my god. My car!" she says.

"Oh shit. What happened?" this voice belongs to Johnny.

I see Mindy pacing the perimeter of her vehicle, taking deep breaths.

"You know what happened. *She* happened."

"Come on. You don't really think—?"

"I told you it was just a matter of time until she pulled some stunt like this."

Who are they talking about? Are they talking about me? It makes my heart flutter to think of Johnny thinking about me.

"Maybe you ran over some glass."

"It's all four wheels, Johnny. That's no accident. She did this on purpose. Can you think of anyone else who has a reason to do something like this to me?"

"Okay. I'll talk to someone about it. I promise."

I smile. Maybe it will be me. Maybe I've finally gotten through to him. Maybe he will talk to me and I can convince him what a bad influence she is.

"Look, I'm sorry, babe," he says. Then I watch as he circles his arms around her waist and draws her into a kiss. I want to throw something at her.

"Let me fix this, okay?" he asks.

"But what about your game? You have to catch the team bus."

"Screw the game."

No. This can't be happening. I was supposed to be there tonight. He was supposed to see me—see me cheering for him on the sidelines—and then her spell would be broken. I have a ticket for the commuter bus in my backpack right now. He can't skip the game.

"Johnny, you can't just—"

"No. This is more important. You're more important," he says, kissing her again. "I don't want you waiting out here alone for a tow truck. If she's willing to do this, who knows what else she might try."

A lot. I'd try anything if I thought it would get her disgusting claws out of the love of my life.

"All right. If you really think it's okay to miss a game?"

"It'll be fine. He barely plays me anyway. Give me two seconds to talk to Coach Lew and then I'll get this taken care of."

My heart sinks. It didn't work. My plan didn't work.

27

THE FOLLOWING MONDAY, ONLY THE fourth week of senior year, there is a rotten fish in my locker. It's from her. I know it's from her. I don't report it. If he's hanging out with her, they'll suspect him too. And I would never try to get him in trouble. But the school counselor must have heard about it anyway because now I'm in her office.

"Greta, we've gotten reports of some inappropriate behavior."

I just stare at her face, which is the color of a cantaloupe rind and just as juiceless. I will not crack. I will not be a tattletale on my one true love.

"Do you know what this is in regards to?"

They always give these little pep talks to the kids who get made fun of. I want to tell her not to bother. He's letting his friends do all this to test me. It's not the same as those other kids.

"I'm fine, really. You don't need to worry about me. I can take care of myself."

She wrinkles her brow. "I'm not worried about you. Should I be? Is there something you'd like to talk about?"

"No," I say.

She takes a deep breath. "Johnny Markham is starting to feel uncomfortable about the kind of attention you're paying to him. He asked me to discuss it with you."

"He's mad at me."

"I don't think he's angry, necessarily, just ... uncomfortable."

"He's not mad?"

"He just wants you to stop sending the letters. It's nothing personal at all, he wanted me to tell you that. He thinks you're a real nice girl, in fact, and doesn't want to hurt your feelings."

A smile tugs at the corners of my mouth. He thinks I'm a nice girl.

"He does?" I say. I need to hear it again, need to be sure.

"That's exactly what he said. Word for word. He doesn't want to hurt your feelings at all or make a big deal about it with the other kids. He just wants the letters to stop."

"Okay," I say.

"Good. Glad we got that straightened out. There are a lot of nice boys at this school, Greta. And you're a real nice girl. I'm sure you'll find somebody new."

She doesn't understand our connection.

I hear what she's trying to tell me. She's telling me to give up. But I won't. Not now. Not when he's finally stopped being angry with me. He's not mad. I want to scream it from the rooftops: HE'S NOT MAD ANYMORE!

The tide has turned. I can feel it. He's tired of the letters, okay. I can understand that. But he sees my persistence. He sees I really am sorry.

Now he needs something bigger. An olive branch. A grand gesture to prove to him once and for all that I really do love him, that the truck driver meant nothing.

I'll figure it out. I have to.

Part Six

My Blake

28

THE NIGHT OF AMBER'S DATE rolls around the following week, after Amber is back to sleeping in our room again for more nights than she's not. Pledging isn't technically over, I guess, but she has a few more free nights than last week.

Blake still hasn't written me back. He's obviously punishing me for failing to pledge Kappa, and I have to be patient until he's ready to forgive me.

Amber is excited as she gets ready, so I try to ignore her. But some people always think everyone is interested in them. Even after I pick up a book and hold it in front of my face, she won't stop talking.

"I didn't want to get tied down to just one guy," she says. "But I don't know. Blake is so amazing. I mean, you saw him. Isn't he amazing?"

"He is," I say.

"Maybe this could go somewhere. You never know, right?"

"Right."

"He's so different from anyone I've ever dated. So strong, so confident. Jesus is he confident. He just knows exactly what he wants, you know?"

Which isn't you, I want to say. "Uh-huh."

"And he's not afraid of anything, especially not me. And I'll tell you, sometimes guys are. I know it's hard to believe, but they're just terrified little boys when it comes to pretty girls," she says. Then glancing at me nervously, she adds, "I mean, you obviously know that."

"Yeah."

"It's the way he talks, I think. Like I'm the only person who exists, who ever existed maybe. Maybe it's just that he's older, more mature, you know? I'm so used to awkward high school boys."

"Sure. That could be part of it." There's so much more to Blake than that. You'd have to be connected to him in the way I am to know it, but he's been that strong and confident and intelligent and loving since the day he was born.

"I like him, Greta. I really do."

It's ridiculous that she thinks he'll choose her. Amber is the kind of girl to have sex with, not date, and certainly not marry. She's pretty, but she'll never have the soul connection we have together. I feel bad for her. When he lets her loose, it will break her heart.

"Okay, wish me luck!"

"Good luck," I say.

She walks out the door. I wait until I hear the elevator ding, then follow.

It's amazing how many easy places there are to hide at the SigUp house. Their back yard has a garage and two gate entrances, but none of them are locked. I walk straight up to the front then slip inside the gate that connects the front yard to the back.

It's a beautiful old mansion, big enough for twenty bedrooms and covered in ivy. The backyard is huge, probably more than an acre, and full of bushes and trees and grass run thin from games of football and wild Saturday nights. My favorite tree is a wide old willow with branches dripping to the grounds. There's a huge hot tub too, inside a pergola under the stars.

There are people talking who I can't yet see, so I press my back against the brick and peek around the corner.

There are guys out there, lots of them, setting a table under my favorite willow tree and raking the leaves and stringing up white bulbs. Every guy is dressed in all black except a red hat shaped like a fleur-de-lis that looks like it's made out of foam. Names are scribbled on the bills of the hats, but they aren't their real names. I know this because one of the guys is Tucker and the bill of his hat says, *Baby Face Barf Boy*. I stifle a laugh. He must be pledging SigUp. They must all be pledges.

Someone whistles and they drop whatever it is they're doing to line up on the sidewalk. From my position here I can only see their backs. I'd like to sneak out to get a better peak, but everyone is so still I know my movement would catch their eye. I stay put, but crane my neck out for a better view.

Just as I do, I see Blake traipse down the back patio steps and walk in front of them. He looks amazing. He's not wearing jeans like most of the guys do. He's wearing pressed blue oxfords and a white button-down shirt. He stops in the middle of the line to face them all.

"Who are your brothers?"

"SigUp SigUp SigUp-Up-UP!" they all chant in unison.

"What do we believe?"

They take a breath almost as one and chant, "Loyalty above all. Service to our brothers. Scholarship and Excellence in all things."

Blake gets a giggle behind his eyes. "And what are you?"

"Maggots."

"What was that?" he laughs.

"MAGGOTS!" they shout.

"That's right. And what do maggots do?"

"Whatever their host commands."

"Your host commands silence tonight until he commands otherwise. Who will speak?"

No one says a word.

"Good," Blake says. "She'll be here any minute. Let's show her how SigUp boys treat a lady. Back to it, maggots. I want everything to be perfect."

They all go back to their tasks.

Are they talking about Amber? Oh, *please.* All of this is for *her*?

It can't be true. He couldn't really believe she's worth all this effort. He must be putting on a show for these guys. Or maybe he's trying to teach them. Yes. He's teaching them, he must be. Boys like Tucker don't have half the presence of a man like Blake. They need to learn from someone who knows how to treat a woman. And this night, these lights strung against the darkness and candles on the table and perfect place settings, all of this is a practice run for me. He wouldn't want to expose me to any sort of mistake, so he's practicing on Amber. If you think about it, it's actually very sweet.

I start composing a letter to him in my mind. It is a nice letter, a love letter. Soft music starts playing and it's growing darker and darker and I know just the words I'll say to him to make him mine.

Then I hear the click of the back door opening.

"Wow," Amber says. "You did all this for me?"

"Don't let it go to your head," Blake says.

Amber laughs. She thinks he's joking, but he's not. I can tell.

"Come on, sit down."

The table is just too far to see from this corner of the house. I tiptoe out, quiet as I can, hoping no one will notice me. Then I settle in behind the hot tub. They can't see me from here. Well, technically they could see me, but only if they were looking. They won't be looking. At least Amber won't. She's oblivious to what all this really is: a lesson. And if Blake notices me (How could he not? I know he feels it too.) If he notices me, he'll know there's no need to practice. I accept him just as he is. I appreciate the effort, though. It's so romantic and so thoughtful of him. My heart soars thinking about all the work he's putting into wooing me.

Tucker slides through the curtain of the branches with a wine bottle and pours her a glass. You can tell it's everything he can do not to say hello to her, not to force her to look up and notice he's there.

When she finally does look up, she says, "Tucker?" then laughs, "Ohmygod Tucker. What are you wearing?"

Tucker straightens up and looks off into the distance. I almost think he sees me. Almost. But he keeps quiet, says nothing.

"Tucker? Hello?" she waves a hand in front of his face, but he still doesn't respond. "What's going on?" she asks Blake, laughing.

"The pledges aren't allowed to talk this evening," Blake says with a grin.

"Ah … okay? That's weird."

"Not really. I had to do it too. It's part of the deal. The price of brotherhood." He turns to Tucker and says, "you can go now. Thank you." Tucker walks out, then Blake turns back to Amber.

"Truthfully? I've been looking forward to this for years. Just wish I could have done it to the guys who initiated me.

They were bastards. Trust me, I'm nice compared to those douchebags."

"Oh, God. Thank goodness the Kappas haven't been that mean to me. I'd never survive it."

"Nor should you have to," he says. "You're far too beautiful for that."

Amber's blush is so bright I can see it, even through the dim light.

Another pledge, this one with *Dickless Darren* scrawled on his cap, rolls out a tray of food.

"I hope you like duck," Blake says.

"Okay, there's no way you cooked this, right? Please tell me you didn't cook this because that would make you a little too perfect."

"You got me. I cannot tell a lie. Nor can I subject you to my cooking," Blake says.

Amber laughs.

"There's a farm to table place on Hampstead that's really great. But I did take it out of the container and put it on a decent plate. Does that count?"

"If we're doing this by points, then yes. Amber zero. Blake about nine thousand."

"I over did it, didn't I?"

"No! No. This is incredible, thank you," Amber says. But she has a funny look on her face.

"You look confused."

"I guess … I thought I'd show up here tonight and we'd have a beer and maybe some pizza or something. Not all this."

"You don't like it?"

How ungrateful of her! After he's gone through all this effort! This is the problem with girls who are given everything when they're growing up. They appreciate nothing. Nothing.

"It's not that," she tries to back-peddle, but Blake can see through it. I know he can. "It's just, why all this effort?" she gets quieter. I barely hear her when she says next, "For me, I mean. I'm just a freshman."

Blake looks at her like he doesn't understand, then that warm smile, the smile he was smiling when I first saw him, spreads across his face.

"Don't talk like that," he says with a grin. "It makes you sound insecure. And you, Amber, have nothing to be insecure about."

29

I CAN'T FIGURE OUT A way to get past the back door once they go inside, probably heading for his bedroom upstairs. All the pledges are milling about, cleaning up, whispering to each other to shut up before somebody comes out. I decide to go back to the dorm room so it doesn't look weird when Amber comes home tonight. *If* she comes home tonight. I wouldn't if I were her.

As I'm tiptoeing out, I hear the crunch of a twig behind me. Tucker is standing there, staring right at me.

"What are you doing here?"

"You're not supposed to talk."

He tilts his head and stares at me and I realize it's not something I should know unless I've been standing here a very long time. "What are you doing here?" he says.

The look in his eye scares me. I don't like it. It's like he's suspicious and hating me and thinking I'm disgusting all at once.

"I don't like you," I say. "You're a bad person and I don't

like you."

"Were you spying on them?"

"No."

"Who is it? Her or him? It's her, isn't it?"

"No! It's not—it's not anyone. Stop saying that! Stop it!"

I pick up a rock and hurl it at him. It misses. I turn and run. Fast, out the gate.

"You're fucking crazy!" he yells after me. I hear another person come up to him.

"What was that?"

I don't look back.

I race and race until I don't know where I am anymore. It's dark and too cold for October. One of those early snows feels like it's in the air, ready to upset the trick-or-treaters who will be out in just a couple of weeks.

A cat darts out of the darkness and stares at me like he knows me, the real me, not the me I am here.

"Shut up," I say.

It looks away, licks the hair off its back, and takes a paw against its tongue to groom it. Maybe it doesn't know.

"Come here, pretty," I say. It comes. Animals love me. They always love me. I pet it and pet it and pet it, so hard there's hair in my hand when I stop. And on my clothes too. That will teach her, I think. She'll sneeze and her eyes will water and she won't know why. I shove the hair into my pocket.

When I get back to the room, there's someone waiting

outside.

"Hey you! I tried to call, but you didn't pick up." It's Aunt Peggy.

"My cell must have been off. Sorry."

"It's okay, I haven't been waiting long. I brought you some coffee. That place on the corner has the best espresso."

"I hate coffee."

"Oh. Okay." The tone of her voice is snippy, like she's just as irritated as I am to be here. "Look, I know you don't want me around, but—"

"Then why are you here?"

"I'd just," she sighs. "I'd appreciate it if you gave me a chance."

"You're just here to spy on me for my mom. We both know that."

"That's not—okay. Okay, I can see how you'd get that impression and I'm sorry if that's the way you feel. But I think there's a big difference between looking out for you and spying on you."

The look in her eyes is sincere. I can feel the love coming off her. It's real, I think. Maybe, maybe, I don't know … It could still be a trick.

"We're family, but we barely know each other," she says. "I'd like a chance to get to know you."

"Okay." It's not an outright agreement, she can hear it in my voice. It's an opening, a tiny crack in the door.

"Why don't we have a little spa day this weekend? My

treat. And no reporting back to your mom, okay?"

"Promise?"

"I promise. I want you to feel like you can trust me. You can, you know. If you need anything."

"I know. I—thanks. Sorry about before. It's been a rough night."

"How come?"

"No reason. It's fine. Just classes and stuff."

"Well, I'd love to talk about it if you'd like? We can go back to the coffee shop and get whatever you want."

"Actually, I think I'd rather just go to sleep. But we can do that spa day on Sunday if you want."

"That would be great."

"Great."

"Okay," she comes in for a hug. "Well, I'll let you get to bed then. Have a good sleep. 'Night."

"Night."

Finally, she goes.

When I go inside, I take the cat hair out of my pocket and stuff it deep inside Amber's pillowcase.

She comes in the next morning around nine, and all her moving around wakes me up.

"What are you doing?" I ask.

"Oh, Greta. I'm sorry I didn't call, but you just would not believe the night I've had. It was so romantic."

I bet I can guess, I want to say.

"Really?" I say instead, tucking into my blankets even

deeper. I don't want to encourage her to share the details. I don't want to hear them.

"It was incredible. He made me this dinner under the stars and then after we ate he—"

RAP. RAP. RAP.

Someone is knocking at our door.

"I wonder if he sent me flowers. That would be so like him," she says. I want to punch her in the face.

She skitters over to the door and opens it. But it's not flowers. It's a cop. Two cops. I sit up in bed.

"Hello, officers. Can I help you with something?" she asks, clearly trying to flirt with them even though she just got home from what she said was an amazing night with Blake.

"Are you Greta Bell, by any chance?"

"I'm afraid not," she says. "Greta, these nice gentlemen would like to speak to you." She turns back to them. "Come on in, boys."

They smile at her. It's sick how easily some men can fall prey to the charms of a siren.

They pull out our desk chairs and sit across from my bed.

"Sorry to bother you so early in the morning, miss. But we have a couple of questions about the fire over at the Tri-Alpha house." The officer speaking is black with skin so dark his eyes demand attention by contrast. He's tall, muscular, and not just a little bit handsome. Still, it doesn't excuse Amber for acting like such a slut around them.

"What about it?" I ask.

"Well, miss, it appears it wasn't an accident."

"But they said it started in the kitchen," I say.

"Well, we've had the report back from the arson investigator. He seems to think differently. And the girls there told us about your little spat that day."

"Were they mean to you, Greta?" Amber asks. "Why didn't you tell me? Everyone says those girls are the worst. They were the first house I dropped."

I look at the officer. "Yeah. They were really mean. I might have—I don't know—I might have called them some names and left pretty quickly."

"That's what we heard," the other officer says. He looks a bit older than his partner, though not by much, and isn't anywhere near as good looking. He's tanned and has blond hair cut close to his scalp, but his eyes are small and it looks like he might have broken his nose at some point and never gotten it fixed.

"We may have gotten into a fight, but I would never want to hurt them," I say. "It wasn't like that."

"Can you account for your whereabouts on the night of the fire?" the white officer says.

"I can account for her whereabouts, officer," Amber says. "We were together the whole night. I remember it specifically because I hadn't seen her all day and we had so much to tell each other."

I look at her in surprise but try to hide it from my face. We weren't together that night. She tried to come, but I made her believe I had a secret date. Either she remembers things incorrectly or she's lying for me.

"You're sure about this?" the black officer asks.

"Absolutely," Amber says.

"Then thank you for your time, ladies. We'll let you know if we have any more questions."

They leave. As Amber closes the door behind her, she whispers to me with a conspiratorial grin. "Please tell me you didn't burn that house down? Because if you did, we're both going to the pokey."

"Of course not," I say with a laugh.

"I know. I'm just teasing. The world is too beautiful today for stuff like that."

Amber crashes into her bed dramatically. Her head lands on her pillow. She sneezes.

30

THE SPA IS AT AUNT Peggy's gym, which is the nicest gym I've ever seen. I didn't even know gyms like this existed. It's all white lacquer and pristine glass with grass-green accents that make it feel fresh and new.

The woman at the front desk, Willow, takes her card and says, "Welcome Ms. Danforth. Did you bring a visitor today?"

"This is my niece, Greta Bell."

"Welcome to WellSpring, Miss Bell. Please let me know if I can be of any assistance during your visit."

"Okay," I say. No one but teachers has ever called me Miss Bell before. She hands me a thick white towel and a fluffy white robe with *WellSpring* embroidered on the chest.

"Oh, we'll drop back by for those," Aunt Peggy says. "We're going to take a Pilates class before our service."

"Excellent. Karen is teaching today. She's amazing. Enjoy yourselves."

Aunt Peggy leads me to a frosted glass door and presses

her pass against a box on the side. A light on the box goes from red to green and there's an electronic *whir-click* before Aunt Peggy pulls the door open.

She leads me into the locker room, which is just as pristine as everywhere else. It smells like lavender everywhere. The lockers are made of real wood—bamboo I think. And everything is clean and minimal. You could eat off the floors in here.

The place is so swanky it gets me wondering what Aunt Peggy does for a living to be able to afford somewhere like this as her regular gym. Back home, any gym at all would have been a luxury. This gym seems like it's exclusively for rich people. It makes me realize how little I actually know about Aunt Peggy. She visited sometimes, but it's hard to get to know someone just from visits.

First we take our Pilates class. I'm bad at it. I keep getting tangled up in the ropes and doing things wrong. But the instructor is nice about it. She laughs off every flub and gets me pointed back in the right direction.

Aunt Peggy is a master, though. She almost looks like a ballet dancer, except older and with a thin layer of flab over all her muscle.

Eventually, when I start to get the hang of things, it feels good. Really good. My body feels strong and elegant at the same time. My toes point and stretch. My muscles ache from the sweet pressure of the pain. I want more of it.

Afterward, we go back through the gym area toward the spa. Willow hands us our towels and robes and Aunt Peggy shows me where to go. It's another area, a whole different section from the gym, but styled the same. There are plush couches and tall plants and orchids everywhere.

We get full body massages and mud wraps and facials. We get manicures and pedicures and absolutely everything the place offers, I think.

"What kind of work do you do, Aunt Peggy?" I finally ask as the manicurist is painting my toes.

"Hmm?" she says from her relaxed haze.

"What do you do for a living?" I say.

"I'm the CFO of a tech company, sweetie," she says. "Have you ever considered that career path? Something in finance? I hear you're a math genius."

"I don't know about that," I say.

"Don't be so modest," she says, seeming suddenly tired. "Girls are always trained to be so modest. It's silly. I saw your SAT scores. I know what you're capable of."

"I never really thought much about what career to pick."

"Well, think it over. It's a great life. I like it at least. Busy, though, not a lot of time for having a family," she says.

Aunt Peggy never got married. My mom always said she thought Aunt Peggy had become a lesbian late in life, but hearing her talk about her work, I'm not so sure. She was probably just married to her job. I don't think it's something I could do. The idea of not having a future with Blake, not getting married and having babies who stare up at me with his beautiful green eyes? I really can't imagine it.

"But there are lots of challenges and plenty of interesting

people. And, of course, you certainly don't have to skip the whole family thing if you don't want to. Plenty of people do both. If you ever feel like taking a tour of my company, just let me know and I'll arrange a visit."

"Okay," I say.

"So what else is going on? How are classes? How's Amber?"

"Good," I say. I'm getting tired of her questions. She's a little too interested in me. But I suppose it's because she doesn't really have a life of her own.

"You guys been up to anything fun?"

"Not really. She's in a sorority now, so she doesn't have much time."

"Ugh. That's too bad. I never liked those girls."

"Exactly. They're terrible people," I say.

"But I thought Amber was really nice?"

"Uh-huh," I say because I know it's what she wants to hear.

"Anyway. What about boys? Met anyone nice yet?"

"One. Sort of. It's not really a big deal," I say, even though it is a big deal. I just don't want Aunt Peggy to ask me any more questions about him. Then, for good measure, I say. "We're taking it slow."

"That's good, honey. There's no rush."

Of course there's a rush. Every moment I'm not with him—every single moment—feels like my heart could stop.

"Right," I say.

After all the spa services are over, Aunt Peggy wants to take a final steam. The club puts eucalyptus into the steam, and it's like being inside a tropical rainforest. We sit in there, in the steam room, cooking in the wet heat.

Aunt Peggy says. "Doesn't it feel good to get your blood pumping like that? With the workout and the massage and the facial and everything? It's probably my favorite thing to do."

"Yeah, it does." It's the truth. I've loved every moment of it. The whole day has been absolutely delicious. Exactly what I needed.

I lay down on the warm tiles and let my towel slip off into the mist. It doesn't matter. We're alone and family and she can't see anything anyway with all this steam. It's warm as a blanket around me and filling up my lungs and making me woozy and happy. I imagine Blake's face breaking through the cloud to kiss me. The hot air on my skin is his hot breath instead. I wish I were alone, totally alone, here.

"I don't know about you, but it makes me think clearer, too."

And when she says it, I realize I am thinking clearer. I'm thinking crystal clear. I can see the way forward like I've never been able to before. I know what to do. I know exactly what to do.

31

WHEN I GET BACK HOME, there's a note from Amber:

> *Sorry, have to run, sorority stuff. And they commandeered my phone! Can't do dinner like we talked about after all. Sorry! Will be gone all night. See you tomorrow! Wish you were here with me!*

There are smiley faces all over it, like little sunshine bombs. As if some stupid smiley face could make things better.

I decide it's okay I didn't get in at the sorority. It would only interfere with my plans. And I'll be in the sorority soon, anyway. At the very latest by next semester. He's punishing me now for not doing it on my own, but Blake will get me in if I want.

Or maybe I won't be a part of them at all. Maybe I won't like that they didn't see my potential when they had a chance. Maybe I'll be too busy being Blake's, all Blake's, to have time for stupid sorority things.

Then it hits me. Amber will be gone all night. *All night.* I can do whatever I want.

I start in her desk. There's not much in here. Her laptop, some stationery with her name printed at the top, and the silver desk set her grandmother gave her as a graduation present. Amber made fun of it after Bunny left. "Who uses a desk set anymore?" she said. Yet another thing she couldn't show gratitude for.

I move on to her closet. Deep in the back of the top shelf there's a shoebox full of old pictures and love letters from her ex-boyfriend. Which is very interesting, don't you think? If she's so in love with Blake, why does she even have these anymore? It makes me glad I have nothing left from Johnny. Except his sweater, but that's not the same. It's just clothes. I don't want anything to remember him by. His deficiencies seem so glaring in the bright light of Blake's incredible whole.

I rifle through the shoebox. There's one picture where she's in a prom dress on her massive staircase at home. I can only tell it's her house because there's a painted portrait of her on the wall. Otherwise, it's so fancy I might think it was a hotel. The guy has his arm around her and she's beaming. It makes me angry how pretty it is. It makes me angry how perfect her dress is and how flawless her hair and makeup are—she must have gone to a salon. Her parents must have paid for everything. It makes me angry how big and grand that staircase is and how sparkling the chandelier above her glows.

How can one person deserve to have so much? Especially someone like Amber, someone who doesn't appreciate anything. Our friendship, Blake's efforts to make her happy—nothing. I spit on the photo. I spit into the box. Then I tear the photo into tiny pieces and scatter the pieces through the box and shove the box, hard, back to where it was on her shelf.

I reach my arm and feel into the shelf. Then I find them. The glasses. The glasses he gave her the night we met. They're just sitting up there like she doesn't care about them at all. If I were her, I would care. Blake doesn't know that about me, not yet, but I would care for everything he ever gave me, not shove it up on a shelf like I never wanted to see it again.

Amber is careless with her things because she thinks things are easy to come by. She has no idea what things cost. I should smash them, that would teach her a nice little lesson, wouldn't it? But just knowing he touched them makes me stop. I put them on instead. They make me feel strong.

I go through Amber's clothes. All her stupid perfect clothes. I take off my clothes and put on her blue dress. Her shoes don't fit me, so I put on a pair of my own. I look in the mirror. I look just as fake as she does.

I rip off the dress. Rip it off. It tears as I strip myself of it, so I stuff it under her bed. If she asks about it, I'll tell her she did it when she was drunk and just doesn't remember it.

She has so many things, she probably won't even miss it. And it's not like the girl never drinks. She's probably spent fewer nights sober than drunk since we got here.

As I'm walking back to my pile of discarded clothes, I catch a glance of myself in the mirror, naked, wearing only his glasses. Something about the image is right. It's so right. Someday he will see me like this. Just like this. Just for him.

I will it to be true. I close my eyes and envision our future together, clear as day.

There's a knock on the door and I'm startled out of my vision. I peek through the peephole to see who it is.

My heart explodes in my chest.

It's Blake. Of course it is.

He can feel it. He can. There *is* a connection between us. I called him here with the pure force of my need for him.

I smooth my hair and open the door.

"Jesus," Blake says.

I've shocked him. I like shocking him.

"You're the one who knocked," I say, mimicking his words the time he showed himself to me.

He looks away, down the hall.

"Is ah, is Amber here?" My heart explodes again, but this time it is with rage. Still? He still wants to punish me?

"She's with the Kappas," I say, leaning up against the doorway and arching my back to show off my best feature.

He's still looking away. "Are you sure? We were supposed to go out tonight."

"She left a note. She won't be back until tomorrow," I say.

Then, "They're not as great as you think, you know."

"What?"

"The Kappas. They're bitches, just like the rest of them."

"Okay, whatever," he says. He looks up to the ceiling, avoiding his eyes like the gentleman he is.

"You don't have to look away. You don't have to do that," I reach for his hand. "And your plans for tonight are ruined, right? Why don't you come inside for a while?"

He pulls his hand away.

"Just tell her I was here, okay?" He starts to leave.

"Amber doesn't appreciate things," I say. "She doesn't know how."

He turns back, a confused look on his face.

"Please don't go. Stay with me." I reach out my hand again, but he doesn't take it.

I drop my hand and open the door wider to let him see all of me. I am here for him. Just for him.

He finally lets himself look at me, really look. His gaze grows cloudy with desire and I can see him fighting to keep his breath even. I can see him shift his stance to hide the bulge in his pants too.

His eyes meet mine and there's a dazzle in them, a glint of amusement at my boldness and pride that I am his.

And I am his. Only his. He deserves all of me.

I close my eyes to remember the look on his face forever. I keep them closed to let him see me, savor me without judgment or pressure. I hear the shuffle of his foot against the carpet and feel the heat of him one step closer, so close that if he reached out, he could touch me.

"Whoa! Sorry!"

It's not his voice. I flash my eyes open and watch as the girl next door shuffles away, laughing.

"I gotta go," Blake says. Then he's gone. I close the door and close my eyes, remembering his face, his scent, his almost-touch.

That night I go out to find more cats.

32

AMBER COMES HOME THE NEXT afternoon, looking tired. Her hair is windblown and her face is pallid except for where someone has pasted temporary tattoos of glittery, gold suns on it.

"Hey," she says.

"How was your night?"

"It was …" her face brightens for a moment, thinking about all the fun she must have had while breaking Blake's heart, standing him up like that. Bitch.

Then she seems to notice the look on my face and decides to keep her comments in check. "It was exhausting. Seriously. You should be glad you didn't have to go through the whole thing." She takes off her shoes.

"Blake came by," I said. "He said you had a date?"

She flops into bed, fully clothed, face into her pillow. "Yeah, he found me."

I panic but try not to let it seep into my voice. "What did he say?"

Could he have told her? No. It was special. Just between us. He wouldn't have shared something so special with her.

"He wasn't mad. He knows how pledging goes."

"Well, that's good." It's not good. Not at all. She stood him up! And he's letting it slide? How could he? It was the perfect excuse. He should've told her it was over. He had a clear out with Amber. She fucked up. He should've used it.

And Amber, so cavalier about all of it. I mean, *come on*.

I'm about ready to call her out on it, tell her exactly what I think of everything she's been doing to Blake: unappreciative, uncaring, neglectful—all the things I would never be. I stand up so I can see her better, so she can see me.

But she's already asleep.

Amber's sleeps horribly the entire week. Every day she wakes up with watery, itchy eyes and the sniffles. No matter how much concealer she puts around her giant orbs (they look like frog's eyes), it doesn't help.

"I know this is a weird question, but you haven't brought any cats in here, have you?"

"Huh? Why would I bring a cat into our room? You're allergic."

"It's just, I get like this when I'm around cats, but I haven't been around any cats so I thought maybe you had."

"No. I don't even like cats."

"I must be coming down with something then. That's so weird."

"Does Blake have a cat?"

"No. Nobody in the house has pets."

"Huh. Crazy." I can't keep the tiniest hint of a smile out of my voice. When I look up, she's giving me a weird look. "What?"

"Nothing," she says.

33

THE NEXT PARTY I ATTEND is harder to get into. It's a mixer at the Kappa house for SigUp guys and no one else is allowed to come. I don't like the idea of this, the two of them alone in a place I can't be. It worries me for Blake. It really does. The more I see Amber, the more I see what a temptress she is. And men—even men who are in love with someone else like Blake is—are so trusting when it comes to girls.

Obviously, I tried to ask Amber for an invitation, but she said there was nothing she could do.

Instead, I go early. Really early. I leave the dorms at four in the morning, tiptoeing past Amber's sleeping form. I sneak into the Kappa backyard before the sun is awake.

It's so girly back here that I'm glad again I wasn't invited to join. There are trellises everywhere covered with autumn colored vines. A long balcony on the second floor creates a full, covered patio below. White iron benches with ornate flourishes are situated in shady spots under the trees, too cold now to enjoy. The effect is both collegial and feminine. To the girls who live here, it's probably a charming downgrade to what they have at home and what they'll eventually attain on their own or through marriage. *Ha-ha! Remember that run-down old garden at the Kappa house? Those were the days!* But to everyone else on planet earth, it is luxurious and opulent.

The wind bites at my appled cheeks. There's snow coming today, the forecast says so, and the gray skies agree. I've bundled up, though, nabbing a thick oatmeal-colored sweater from Amber's dresser that she'll never miss. I'm ready for the day.

What I'm not ready for is how to get inside. I try the back door, hoping it was accidentally left unlocked overnight, but it doesn't budge. The front door is the same, as are all the windows on the ground level. No one has been as careless as I expected.

But there must be a way. I circle the house one more time, slowly, looking at every possible way inside. There's only one other way I can see and it won't be easy. I need to get up to that balcony.

I go around to the west side, the side where there's a trellis going from the ground all the way up to the balcony. It's dripping with thorny vines, probably the remnants of overly-perfumed climbing roses. The trellis looks old. Once bright white, its paint is peeling and faded and chipping off from the rub of the branches. I shake it a little to see if it will hold, and the easy movement makes me uneasy. But I don't see any other options. The sun is on the horizon now, and if I'm going to do this, I need to do it now—before anyone wakes up. This will work. It has to.

I take a tentative grasp of the wood and hoist myself up. It creaks against my weight, but it holds. I climb up a few more steps until I'm at least six feet off the ground. Even at that height it would hurt to fall. I grip tighter and the wood groans. I need to keep moving.

As I'm reaching for my next handhold, a gust of wind whirls past, throwing me off balance. It whips my body away from the trellis until I'm hanging in the air like a flag waving in the breeze, only one hand and one foot making contact. There's a big creak this time, the grating sound of steel against wood, screws working their way out of their anchors.

Panicking, I swing my body back and clench a hold with my free hand, but it hits a thorn and I have to stifle a wail. I reposition my hand to an open spot, take a deep breath, and continue up.

There's a snap underneath me.

My left foot crashes free, the rotted wood underneath it giving way. I hold on tight and shove my foot into another diamond in the trellis. The wood groans all around me now, from the wind and my weight and the ghosts of the roses that once lived here.

Faster is better. I need to go faster. I need to get this over with. I hurl myself upward, heedless of the thorns, more scared now of falling than tearing my delicate skin.

I am five feet from the top.

Four feet.

Three.

With a last push, I scramble over the carved stone railing and thud to the cold tiles of the balcony. My breath is coming in hard gasps now, billowing out into white clouds in front of me, and my hands are bloodied from the climb. But I made it up.

The adrenaline pumping through my veins screams victory, but it's not over yet. I'm up, but I still need to get inside.

I get to my feet and tiptoe over to the French doors that open onto the balcony. I peer through the sheer curtains to see where the doors lead, but it's dark inside, too dark to see anything.

I turn the handle slowly and it doesn't protest against my force. It's unlocked.

I pull the door back, molasses slow and feather light. There's a tiny *screech* from the hinges and I stop, go slower, until it's wide enough to walk through.

I step inside and shut the door softly behind me.

I stand perfectly still until my eyes adjust to the darkness. I'm at the end of a hallway. All around me are doors to bedrooms where Kappas sleep soundly. There's not a sound, not a voice or footsteps to be heard. It's still early, still before five, and most of these girls were probably out partying last night. Now that I'm inside, I have plenty of time.

I walk forward about fifty feet until I arrive at a wider open space with a large wood balustrade. I'm standing on the upper landing of the grand staircase. Below me is the foyer Claire led me into for the first time so many weeks ago, where those bitches chose Amber instead of me. It doesn't matter. I'm better off. Freer. I'm sure of it.

I tiptoe down the steps. Past the foyer is another hall that leads back to the kitchen. It's a big kitchen, classically designed with white cabinets and white marble countertops and appliances that look industrial. The refrigerator is double-sized and the pantry is enormous. Both are stocked with enough organic food to fuel a health club.

I wonder if they have a full-time chef. They probably do. I'll have to ask Amber. I steal some snacks—an apple and some cheese and a bottle of spring water. I could be waiting a while.

Off the kitchen is a huge formal dining room with several round tables covered with white linen tablecloths and set with fresh flowers. There are enough chairs to seat a hundred girls at least, maybe more. At the front of the room hangs the Kappa coat of arms, split three ways with the words "truth," "elegance," and "virtue" scrawled in each pie.

Amber had to memorize all kinds of stupid chants about it. I heard her doing it in the bathroom. But when I came inside she stopped. She acted like it was a big important secret or something and not just a lame hoop they were making her jump through like a trained pig.

Under the coat of arms is a rectangular table that looks like it's for the important people. Probably the president, Alexis, and her crew because the chair in the middle is the biggest in the whole room. And the ones beside it are more ornate too. Maybe she thinks of herself as a queen, not a president. Amber certainly seems to worship her. The whole idea of the inner-workings of this place strikes me as utterly ridiculous. I have to stifle a laugh.

Against the wall is another rectangular table, but this one is narrower and covered with large chafing dishes. This is the place. Everyone gravitates toward the food. I tuck myself under the table and get comfortable.

34

THIS WAS A MISTAKE. I shouldn't have planted myself under here. Everyone's moving around so much. I can barely hear anything to begin with, and I'm pretty sure Blake hasn't come within ten feet of me all day. I thought I heard him once, his hearty laugh booming across the room, but I couldn't hear any of the words. Now I'm stuck, maybe until this thing is over. Maybe until tonight. I'm tired from waking up so early and my body aches from being crunched underneath here so long. My food ran out two hours ago. So did the water, which was another mistake because now I have to pee too.

Just as I'm about to give up and try to figure out a way to escape my hiding place and find a bathroom, I hear a voice. Amber's voice.

"So how do you like SigUp?" she's asking someone.

"I can't complain," a guy says. His voice is deep and sort of gravely. I don't recognize it. "You're incredibly beautiful. Has anyone ever told you that?"

"Once or twice," she laughs flirtatiously. "But I can't say it ever gets old."

She's flirting with him. She's actually flirting with him when Blake is right here in the same room! What a total slut.

"Let me take you out," he says. "Drinks, food, whatever you want."

"That's probably not the best idea. I'm sort of already seeing one of your brothers."

"That's okay. We don't mind sharing."

Gross. Of course, Amber invites this kind of attention. He must be able to tell from her expression that she'd do it. I know she would. If Blake let her, she'd probably spread her legs for anyone.

"You're a real charmer," she says with a snort. "I mean, how could a lady pass up an offer like that?"

"So who's the lucky guy?" he asks.

"Blake Abbott?" she says.

"Fuck. Nevermind," he says. "I'm really sorry, okay?"

"Okay?" she says, her voice lilting up and stretching out at the end like what he just said is weird. "Not a big deal."

I hear the sound of him walking away.

"Well, that was bizarre," she says.

Then more footsteps, hard ones, coming closer.

"What was that about?"

It's him! It's my darling Blake! And he saw everything. He must have.

"You're boy over there was laying the moves on pretty

thick," Amber says.

She wanted him to, I want to scream. *She wanted him to!*

"Why?" Blake asks. "Did you say something to him?"

My heart leaps in my chest. Maybe he's finally seeing her for what she really is.

"No," she laughs. "I'm pretty sure I scared him off. I don't think he knew we were seeing each other."

"I find that hard to believe," he says. "Don't worry. I'll speak to him."

"You really don't have to do that," she says.

"Yes, Amber. I do."

"Wow," Amber laughs. "Somebody's jealous."

"Why would I be jealous of him? He's a fucking pledge."

"You *are* jealous!" she giggles. I see the shadow of her legs behind the tablecloth, watch her feet move between his. "What are you gonna do? Throw me over your shoulder and carry me back to your cave?"

"Maybe," he says.

Then I hear her gasp, gasp like he just did something. Is he touching her? I can't see anything. I can't tell what's happening. I move my head closer to their feet and pull the tablecloth up slow, slow, slow. Just two inches, but I can see his hand is up her skirt. I can see her looking around the room to see if anyone can see.

"Blake—" she says, her voice breathy and soft. It sounds like part warning, part plea.

"Is that what you want me to do? Carry you over my shoulder?" he asks, his voice low and sexy. "Have my way with you?"

"Mmm-hmm," she says. The sound of her like that, tempting him with her voice, makes me want to vomit. I let the tablecloth drop.

Then they're trotting away to who knows where and my heart is broken. She tricked him again. The fucking hussy tricked him *again*. Some women are shameless.

I want to follow them, to tell Blake everything, but I can't. I'm stuck under here. It's all I can do not to scream.

The minutes pass slowly after they're gone. So slow it could be hours. And it's so warm. Too warm. The chafing dishes must have been lit two hours ago, but they're still burning. The heat is making me woozy and the smell of all that rich food is making my stomach churn. I need to take off some of my layers, but there's not a lot of room under here to maneuver.

If I don't, though, I'll pass out.

I lay down on the ground, stretching myself under the length of the table, trying not to make the tablecloth wave as I do. Inch by inch, I slide Amber's oatmeal sweater up my body, past my chest, and over my head. When I finally get it off, I can feel the tiniest of breezes reaching under the table to cool me. It's so much better. So is being able to stretch my body out like this.

I tuck my coat under my head as a pillow and push the sweater under my backside where it aches from the hard floor. The minutes continue to tick, tick, tick away as the room goes quieter and quieter.

I don't even notice falling asleep.

There's a clang and I wake up with a start, gasping. The gentle clatter of the party is gone, and the light feels different too—stronger and brighter and directly on me somehow. The white tablecloth glows with it.

There's a rustling above my head and the ting of metal against metal.

"You guys really did an excellent job today, thank you. Everyone loved the beurre blanc." I think the voice belongs to Alexis.

"Did they? I'm glad to hear it." This is a voice I don't know. Maybe the chef?

"Hey, do you smell something funny?"

"Like what?"

"I don't know. Something rotten? You don't think we have mice again do you?"

I smell it too. With horror, I realize it's coming from my own body. There's a wet spot between my legs. I couldn't hold it.

"I haven't noticed anything in the kitchen," the chef says.

"Huh. It does smell weird in here, though. Don't you think?" Alexis says.

"It's probably just the linens. Who knows what got spilled on them with all the people in here. I'll get these in the laundry and put out fresh ones."

Shit shit shit shit shit shit shit. I have to get out of here. I have to get out of here now.

"Thanks, Thomas. You're the best."

"No problem."

I hear the clang of dishes in the kitchen and then Alexis' footsteps receding across the carpet in the opposite direction. Then the clack of them again as she hits the hardwood in the foyer.

I peek out from under the tablecloth. There's not a clear view of the room from here, but what I can see is empty. I'll have to take the chance. Who knows how long I'll have until someone else shows up? Or until they pull off the tablecloth and discover me underneath it?

I decide to go for it. I dart out from under the table and get my bearings. Which way to go? The back door is closer, but I'd have to pass by the kitchen, and I can hear somebody in there, washing up. The front door is farther, and I don't hear anything from that direction, but there's a bigger chance of running into someone coming down the stairs or coming in the door.

Then the decision is made for me. Out of the corner of my eye, I see a man dressed in a chef's coat coming out of the kitchen. I dash toward the front door.

I don't even look up as I race through the foyer, yank the door open, and run outside. All I can do is hope no one saw me. I run down the porch, through the yard, onto the sidewalk. Then I chance a backward glance.

No one said anything. No one is chasing after me and no one is coming up the front walk. I keep running, the faster I can get away from this place, the better.

I run and I run and I run. Down the block, around the corner, all the way back to the dorms. I love the adrenaline that's coursing through me right now. I feel alive again, strong, invincible. They didn't invite me, but I came anyway. Not everything is up to them. Sometimes you have to take your fate into your own hands.

My bed feels like the best place on earth when I finally fall into it.

35

IT'S HALLOWEEN AND I'M AT the big SigUp Halloween party. I didn't need an invitation. They let all the hot girls in, and I am hot now. Men can't stop looking at me in my sexy mermaid costume, its green fishtail skirt and hot pink seashell bikini top a perfect balance to my fiery red hair. But I'm not for them. I'm for Blake.

I don't know why I wasn't formally invited. That's not true. I do know. Amber didn't want me here. She's been inviting me to fewer and fewer events lately. She pretends it's just coincidental, that she's busy or it's Kappa-only stuff, but I know better. She feels threatened by me. It's so clear it's laughable.

Blake probably asked her about me, probably asked her to invite me just so he could see me tonight, even for a little bit. But once again, her selfishness got in the way. She doesn't know it, but she couldn't bear to have his real, one true love there while she pathetically tries to make him happy. She has no idea what love is.

But it doesn't matter. I am here. I will surprise Blake and he'll be so overcome he'll have no choice but to leave Amber all alone.

I wander through the crowd, dodging slutty maids and slutty cheerleaders and slutty Greek goddesses. One girl is dressed as a slutty Hawaiian hula dancer, but her grass skirt is so sparse and her coconuts so small it's almost obscene. She might as well be wearing nothing at all. I look a little closer and see the girl is Jessica James, my old Rho Chi. My eyes roll without even thinking about it. And as if she's trying to make her slutty outfit even more cliché, she seems totally trashed already—walking wobbly with a bottle in her hand and slurring her words. Some people have no class.

She's such a train wreck I almost miss it. Out of the corner of my eye, I catch a glimpse of him. First his face and then the whole picture. It's so perfect I want to cry. Tight royal blue pants and a matching blue tunic with a bright red sash. He's a prince. My prince. He must have known what my costume would be. He must have.

But just as I'm about to walk up to him, I see her, Amber, and realize Blake isn't dressed for me at all. She's in a flowing pink princess dress, far shorter and lower-cut than it should be. Her heels are so high and she's wearing white thigh-high's that make her look like a prostitute. Her long blond hair is bouncing in loose curls around her face, and there's a gold-pointed crown on her head. She's Sleeping Beauty. A slutty, disgusting, totally inappropriate Sleeping Beauty.

I disappear back into the crowd. Tonight, I decide, I will just watch. I will watch and let him come to me. Amber's costume is so desperate it shouldn't take long.

Some guy hands me a drink and I guzzle it down. He tries to dance with me, but I say I have to go to the bathroom. I don't go to the bathroom. I wander around the house, memorizing the place Blake calls home, looking for pockets of darkness to hide in and trying to remember it's dangerous to stand in one spot too long. Amber might see me, and I really don't want to talk to her tonight.

As I'm going back for my second drink, I see that Blake is at the drinks table. And he's alone—without Amber. I make a beeline for him, but before I get there, f-ing Jessica James stumbles between us.

"Come to beddy-bye?" she says to him, throwing her arms around his neck and pouting her lips. "Jessie's tired."

"Stop it, Jessica," he says, peeling her arms off and grabbing two cups from the table. One must be for Amber.

He tries to walk away, but she doesn't let him pass. "Please, baby? I need you tonight."

A flash of anger passes over his face. He tosses the cups toward the sink on the bar. Their contents splash everywhere, but no one seems to be looking but me. The music is too loud, the people too drunk. I pretend to sip on my cup and check my phone so he doesn't notice me watching. Looking around, he grabs her by the arm and hauls her into an empty hallway. It looks like the entrance to a back staircase that's so narrow it was probably originally used only by servants. I follow, pressing my back against the wall just outside the entrance so I can listen.

"I told you this had to stop," he says.

"I miss you," she says, her voice all breathy. I peek into the hallway and see he has her wrists pinned above her head. She arches her back so far I think her breasts are going to pop right out of her coconuts.

"You're fucking wasted," he says.

"Isn't that how you like me?"

She leans in and smothers his mouth with hers.

I want him to smack her. I want him to tell her to stop again, put her in her place. But he doesn't. He lets her kiss him for so long I don't know what's happening anymore. And with his free hand, he yanks the coconuts up so her breasts bounce out of the bottom, fully exposed. He kneads them, squeezes them hard, and pinches her nipples. His leg splits hers apart, and she's gyrating against him. Then he presses himself against her so hard I can't tell who is kissing who anymore.

Finally, he pulls away. "Fuck." He slaps the wall with his free hand, right next to her face, still not releasing her wrists. "Fuck, Jess. I won't let you ruin this for me."

I relax. He told her no. She tried to tempt him, but he told her no. I couldn't be prouder of him.

"You fell for her, didn't you?" she asks. I can hear the tears she's holding back, but I don't feel sorry for her. She brought it on herself.

He lets go of her wrists. "Yeah," he says. "I did."

She tugs the bra back over her breasts, takes a deep breath, pastes on a smile. "Then I'm happy for you."

"Thanks, Jess. You're the best." He takes one step away from her.

"But Blake?"

He turns back.

"If it doesn't work out, you'll call me, right?"

"Oh, it'll work out," he says.

"But if it doesn't?"

Suddenly, he's pressed up against her again, diving a hand between her legs, his middle finger extended. Jessica yelps in pleasure, closes her eyes as his hand moves in and out. I hate seeing it, but I can't look away—can't help but imagine it's me against that wall, me he's touching like that.

"You'll know if it doesn't work out," he says. Then he pulls his finger out of her and shoves it in her mouth. She sucks it like a baby with a pacifier, licking herself off him until he takes it away. "Bye, Jess."

She's still up against the wall with her eyes closed when he walks right by me and stops.

"You're a dirty girl, aren't you?" he asks, his voice hushed. He knew I was there, watching the whole time. It was a test. He was testing me.

I look into his eyes, nod.

"You like to watch?" he asks.

"I like to play more," I say, wishing I could touch him, wishing he would touch me.

"But you won't tell?" he asks.

At first, I don't know what he means. Then I realize he's talking about Amber. He doesn't want her to know about this. I don't understand why. It must be another test. But … does he want me to say I won't tell or did he do all of this so I would—so she would leave him and we could be together? Something about his voice tells me he needs me to trust him, needs me to let him take the lead.

"No," I whisper. "I won't tell."

It's what he wanted me to say. I can see I chose correctly the moment the words pass my lips. It ignites a fire behind his eyes.

"Good girl," he says. Then he walks away.

36

AFTER SEEING HIM WITH JESSICA, I don't see him alone again. He seems stuck by Amber's side. I catch small glances of them here and there, but they're never in a place where I can watch them for long without being noticed, so I have to wander.

Eventually, they head to the basement and I follow.

There's a big rec room down here. A Ping-Pong table, a couple of pool tables, video games and couches, a giant flat screen. The whole room is painted glossy black with white horizontal pinstripes, like a vintage racecar. Music echoes from the TV, some video playlist that's more chill than the pumping rhythm from the speakers upstairs. It's more relaxed down here, even though it seems like there are twice as many people per square foot.

Blake winds Amber through the crowd and toward one of the pool tables in the back, where five guys are playing a game. One of them, I think, is Tucker, but I'm not sure. Whoever it is wears a lewd banana costume with an unpeeled, felt banana growing out of his crotch. I can't hear what Blake is saying, but all the brothers who were playing on the table clean up their game and leave. He's powerful here—the president of the fraternity. It's easy to see they all respect him.

I need to get closer so I can hear what's going on. From my wanderings around the house, I've noticed you can get into the storage room from the utility room. The storage room door has a separate entrance, right near them and perfect to observe from if I open it a crack. I head in the opposite direction and into the utility room, then through it into the storage room. There's so much liquor in here the whole fraternity could be drunk for months. I nab a bottle of gin and go to the door, cracking it open as silently as I can.

Amber and Blake are entwined against the pool table, alone now despite the crowd in the rest of the basement. She's leaned over the table, her ass exposed for anyone to see and only covered by what appear to be the tiniest pair of panties I've ever seen. Why even bother with wearing undergarments at all? He lines his body up behind hers, guiding her hand as she makes a shot. I've seen Amber play pool in the dorm lounge. She doesn't need any help. She just wants Blake to see her ass. Women are so devious sometimes. It's really not fair to men.

Amber takes the shot and the balls scatter against the green felt, cracking against each other as they tumble into pockets. She tries to step back, but Blake is still behind her.

He turns her, lifts her onto the table instead, and presses himself between her legs. They kiss.

Amber breaks away from him and giggles. “Your turn.” The cadence of her seduction makes me sick. I can see exactly what she’s doing, trying to play cute and helpless, even if Blake can’t see it.

Blake takes the cue from her and leans over the table. His line is elegant and strong at the same time. When his cue strikes the ball, it makes me gasp it’s so sharp and I’m worried for a moment that they’ve heard me. But the red ball rolls into a pocket just in time to distract them.

“Ooh, nice one!” Amber says.

Blake yawns, “This is kind of boring, don’t you think?”

“I’m having fun.”

Blake pulls her close, “We could have more fun than this. Come on. Let’s go upstairs.”

Amber kisses him back. “Later. Becky and Max will be here soon.”

Blake kisses her again, “I’m sure Becky and Max can find a way to entertain themselves without us.”

Amber pulls away. “It’s barely nine o’clock, Blake.” She looks irritated, then softens. “I thought we were going to have fun tonight.”

“You don’t think I’m fun?” He says to her sexily.

She grins, looks him in the eye, “Of course I think you’re fun. I was just really looking forward to hanging out with Becky tonight. I really want to get to know her better. We’re sisters now.”

Blake pulls away, and I can tell this bothers him. He has a right to be upset. If someone as magnificent as Blake wants you in his bed, how can you refuse him? Her stupidity and selfishness are astounding sometimes.

"If that's what you want," he says.

"Don't be mad."

"Why would I be mad?"

"Oh, Blakey. You are mad."

He stands up tall and beams at her. "Not in the least," he says, then leans in to kiss her, "Just promise me you won't drink too much this time, okay? I want all of you later."

She kisses him back. "Oh, you'll have all of me."

"Promise?" he asks, cupping her ass.

"Every last bit."

"Watcha doin'?" the voice comes from behind me and I jump, dropping the bottle of gin on the floor. It smashes and the liquid mixes with the broken glass and spreads into a clear pool against the concrete. There's yellow in the reflection, banana yellow.

"Just grabbing a drink," I say.

"Something interesting going on out there?" It's Tucker. He takes a step toward me.

"Careful! The glass. Can you get me a towel or something?"

He pushes past me anyway, opens the door. "Yeah, that's what I thought."

The opening door catches Blake and Amber's attention.

"Did you need something, Baby Face?" Blake says.

"No sir. I mean, I think this girl is spying on you two again."

"I was just getting a drink," I say.

"Greta?" Amber is staring at me, confused.

"Hey, Amber."

"What does he mean 'again'?" she says to Blake.

"Your guess is as good as mine," I say.

"I didn't know you were coming tonight. Why didn't you say anything?" Amber says.

"I wasn't sure I'd be here. I had kind of planned on going somewhere else, but it ended up being really lame."

Tucker breaks in, "I bet."

"Jesus, Tucker, I was just getting a drink. The door was already open. It's not a big deal."

"And what were you 'just' doing the other night in the backyard?"

I don't say anything, but my heart is pounding out of my chest.

"What's he talking about, Greta?" Amber says.

"Don't ask me. I have no idea," I say.

"Seriously?" Tucker says. "You're seriously going to play dumb?"

My eyes search desperately for Blake's. He steps in, giving me a look that calms me instantly. "I'll take care of this. Why don't you go back to the party, Tucker?"

"Okay, man. Whatever." Tucker bananas his way past the pool table and up the basement stairs.

"What's going on here?" Amber says.

"We can talk about it later," Blake says. "Greta—"

I love it when he says my name. Just the word in his mouth makes my knees weak.

"There's plenty to drink upstairs. Why don't you go have one of the guys make something special for you?"

I hesitate, hating the idea of leaving him. But it's what he wants. I have to trust him.

"You know what? Find Charles. I think you've met Charles, right? That time at the diner?"

He remembers me from the diner. I nod yes. This is a message. A secret message between only us.

"Tell him Blake said to make you a Sweetheart Punch. It's amazing. You'll love it."

His eyes seem to be sending me a secret message. *Later*, he says. *Our time will come*, he says. *Do as I ask and you will be rewarded*, he says.

"Okay. I guess I'll see you guys later," but I'm only looking at Blake.

"Bye," Amber says.

As I'm walking away, I hear her whisper to Blake, "Can you please tell me what just happened?"

He whispers back, but I can't hear the words.

37

"BLAKE SAID TO MAKE ME a Sweetheart Punch," I say to Charles, who's hovering near the drinks table.

"Oh he did, did he?" he says. Charles is even tanner and sun-bleached blond than he was the last time I saw him.

"Yes," I say, defensive, crossing my arms over my chest, which he's blatantly staring at. "He did."

"Okay, no need to get upset. Why don't you relax over there and I'll bring it to you."

That's better. He should know how to treat Blake's best girl.

I sit down on the last unoccupied cushion on the couch, nudging my way in past a couple making out all sloppy and drunk. I think they're dressed as pirates, but all the grinding against each other makes it hard to tell.

Charles comes back and hands me a drink. It is bright blue and smells fruity and sweet. I love sweet. Blake must have known.

I take a huge swallow of the brew and cough. It's strong.

So strong. Too strong for me but Blake wants me to have it, so I chug it down.

"Thatta girl," Charles says. "You feel like dancing?"

"Not really," I say, a little woozy. I can feel the booze sliding into my bloodstream like I poured it directly into my veins.

"Oh, come on. Everybody likes to dance." He breaks into a stupid move, something that looks like a cross between the moonwalk and a bunny hop. "Don't you like to dance?"

"I love to dance, but not with you. I only want to dance with Blake."

"Oh, right. Of course. Yeah. He told me he really wants to dance with you tonight, but that I should keep you company until he can get away. Come on, dance with me. Just as friends, I swear."

If Blake has asked him to look out for me, then he won't be mad if I dance with someone else, will he? No. He wants me to. Blake sent me to Charles, and Charles said so.

"Okay," I say and stand, even though I'm really not in the mood.

"Perfect!"

Charles leads me out onto the dance floor. My legs feel a little wobbly, a little unsure, but Charles holds me up. Then the beat enters my heart and we're dancing, wild and free.

I think of Blake. I dance for him. I concentrate hard and will him to come up the stairs and see me, see my hair tossed in the air, see my face flecked with light from the disco ball. It's magic, all of this. The drink, the dance, Blake so near. My dance is a spell, a spell for him to come to me.

I look up at the glittering orb and the room spins. I see it before I feel it, the whirl of the lights, Charles' face as he catches me in his arms, holds me close, leans in to kiss me.

"No," I say. "Blake won't like—"

I try to pull myself away from him, but my limbs have gone soft. My voice too.

"Shhh," Charles says. "It's okay. Everything's fine, baby. Blake knows. He asked me to take care of you tonight. Make you happy."

Then he puts his mouth on mine, plunges his tongue between my lips.

I try to tell him to stop. I try to tell him Blake wouldn't like it. Because no matter what Charles says, Blake can't want me to kiss someone else. I won't make the same mistake I made with Johnny. I try to tell him no, but the words won't form on my lips.

Then I feel the heft of his arms underneath me. I feel the bounce of my head against his back. I see the floor, his feet moving underneath us both. I hear the laughter in the room. At me?

There's a jiggle. Stairs. A door. A bed. Black spots under my lids.

Feeling heavy. So heavy.

Then Charles, naked above me.

My fishtail on the floor as the room goes into blotchy darkness.

Then nothing.

38

WHEN I WAKE UP THE next morning, everything hurts. My mouth feels fuzzy and my thoughts are blurry. I look around to see where I am and realize it's not a room I recognize. Next to me, Charles is passed out. His mouth is slack, drool pooling on the pillow under his head. It must be his room. What happened last night? Did Charles let me sleep in his bed? Did Blake ask him to do that? Something about all of it seems wrong, but I can't think clearly enough to piece it all together.

I sit up and it all comes flooding back to me, so fast and so hard I want to vomit.

The Sweetheart Punch. It was so strong, and I drank it all.

The fuzzy feeling in my mind.

The way my body feels sore, the wrong kind of sore.

What have I done?

I realize only then that I am naked. My Halloween costume is scattered across Charles' room in bits and pieces

—my fishtail, my shell bra, my shoes, my purse. And Charles, laying next to me, is naked too.

I've ruined everything. I tried so hard this time, tried to be true to Blake, but I failed his last test.

I should have stopped drinking.

I should have stopped.

I should have stopped.

I stand and rummage through Charles' desk until I find a pen and a piece of paper. Then I scribble Blake a note. Maybe if he sees it first thing when he wakes up, it will help. What else can I do but try?

Dear Blake, My Darling,

I'm so sorry. So very sorry. Can you ever forgive me? You must, you must, you must.

You tested me and I failed, failed in the worst possible way. I am nothing. I am pond scum. I am the dog shit stuck to the bottom of your shoe that you keep smelling all day long and wish you could wash off but you can't. You just can't. Please don't.

I didn't want to be with him. I wanted to be with you. But it was him that I woke up with this morning, his breath rotten and slimy against my cheek. At first I thought, I hoped, it was you. But it wasn't. It wasn't.

How could I do such a terrible thing? How could this have happened? I don't know. I really don't.

I deserve to be punished. Assign me any penance you want. Just tell me even your tiniest wish. I will do anything to make it up to you.

I already am. The real punishment is in my heart. Can you ever come back to me?

I don't need much. Just you. Just your love, whatever way you can give it to me now. I am yours.

Your Greta

Your Love

Your Darling

When I'm done writing it, I walk down the hall and shove it under Blake's door. Amber is probably there with him, sleeping where I should have slept last night. Where, perhaps, I would have slept if I hadn't gotten so drunk I completely lost my judgment. I wonder for a moment if it will be she who finds the note. But I don't care if she does. Blake asked me to keep Jessica a secret, not us. And this is more important. He must have heard about what I did. He has to hear how sorry I am.

A door opens downstairs and someone walks into the house. The breeze from outside makes me realize I still haven't dressed. I'm standing in the hall completely naked. I race back to Charles' room to get my things.

I grab my costume and my purse, checking to make sure my phone is still there. It is. But as I go to put on the bra, I stop. I just don't feel like doing a walk of shame this morning—especially not in my Halloween costume. I can't handle it today if people point and laugh. I just want to disappear for a little while.

I look in Charles' dresser for some clothes. But the top drawer isn't holding any clothes at all. Just some pipes and wrapping papers and a bag of marijuana. There are also two large bongs, a vaporizer, and an old cookie tin without a lid. Inside the tin are hundreds of white, round pills—blister packed in groups of thirty or so. It looks like the way cold medicine is packaged.

I spot the corner of a white box buried under the silver sheets of pills and pull it out. Large blue letters on the box say, *Rohypnol.*

Rohypnol.

Ruffies.

That's how he did it. It wasn't that I drank too much. He put something in my drink. And there's no way, absolutely no way Blake meant for him to do that. He took advantage. Of Blake's kindness, of his trust. He took advantage of me.

That motherfucker.

That stupid, stupid motherfucker.

I find a backpack in his closet and dump all the pills inside, along with my costume. He won't do this to anyone else ever again. Then I find an old pair of basketball shorts, a cap, and a T-shirt and throw them on. My heels will have to do.

As I'm leaving, I remember the note. The goddamned note. It's all wrong—an admission of guilt when there was none, not really. I have to get it back. But when I try Blake's door it won't turn. It's locked.

"Hello?" someone calls up the stairs. "Who is that?"

I go the other direction, race down the back stairwell—the one where Blake was hiding with Jessica last night, then out the back door.

There's only one thing on my mind as I leave the house.

He will pay for what he did.

Charles will pay.

39

IT DOESN'T TAKE ME LONG to decide what to do. The solution is so simple, so easy, that it actually feels elegant.

The same night, I run into Charles casually at a bar. Or rather, I make it look casual. It took a bit of research to find out he was going to be here tonight, but Amber leaves her computer unlocked all the time. And her Facebook was up when she went to go take a shower this morning. I had a pretty good idea of his plans by the time she came back to our room.

"Oh hey," I say, sitting on the bar stool right next to him. "I didn't know you were going to be here."

"You took off pretty quick this morning. Didn't say goodbye," he says. He looks a little wary of me. I'm probably not the first girl to confront him the morning after. But my methods are a bit different.

"Yeah, sorry about that. I was a little embarrassed. I clearly had way too much to drink last night and I get the worst morning breath after I drink. But I remember having some fun before I passed out," I say with a sly grin. "I mean, we did have fun, right?"

"Damn straight," he says, letting his eyes roll over my body appreciatively. I've made an effort to look spectacular tonight—tight skirt, low-cut top, my legs shiny with lotion—and it's working.

I giggle, "I'm really sorry—and please don't be offended—but I sort of can't remember your name."

He laughs. "Shit, I'm glad I'm not the only one. I'm Charles."

"That's it! I knew it was a C name."

"And you are?" he asks.

"Greta," I say.

"Greta. That's right. Can I buy you a drink?"

"Sure."

I order a beer, unscrew the cap myself. There's no need for a repeat of last night. Tonight is all about revenge.

We make small talk for a while. He tells me all about himself—born with a silver spoon, blah, blah, blah. I don't really listen. I don't really care. When he asks about me, I lie. I tell him my parents made their money in tech, that we have a beach house in Silicon Valley, and that I have my own apartment on Downing. I'm just biding my time. He'd be suspicious if I asked too quickly. But after his third beer and my second, I do it.

"Do you want to come back to my place?" I ask. "I've got a six pack cooling in the fridge."

I don't even have a fridge.

"Yeah. Sure," he says.

I tell him I'll drive and we get into my car. Almost immediately, he slides a hand up my skirt and rubs my crotch.

"God, I've wanted to feel where those legs ended," he says. It takes everything in me not to punch the asshole right in the face.

Instead, I giggle and move his hand into his own lap. "Patience. Not while I'm driving."

He smirks while I start the car.

"There's a bottle under the seat if you're thirsty," I say.

He grins, reaches down, and pulls out a bottle of blue liquor. It had to be blue. When I tested it this afternoon, the pills made everything I put them in blue. Which explains the color of the sweetheart punch last night.

"Raspberry vodka?" he asks. "You're such a girl."

"Shut up," I say. "Try it. If you don't like it, then I'll do whatever you want tonight."

"And if I do like it?"

"Then I get to do whatever I want to you."

His eyes go wide. He doesn't say anything else, just takes a big swig. It only takes twenty minutes for Rohypnol to start working and there are enough pills in there to tranquilize a horse. But I've seen him naked. I don't think his dick really qualifies.

"Drink more," I say. "You can't form an opinion on just that."

He laughs, drinks again.

"So?" I ask.

"I think," he says, "that you get to do whatever you want to me tonight."

"That's exactly what I thought you'd say."

Fifteen minutes later he's already talking funny. I pull into the alley behind the SigUp house and lead him through the back gate. He's stumbling and heavier by the second.

"Whadjou do to me?" he asks. It's the fifth time he's asked. "Whadjou do?"

I just barely get him into the gazebo that holds the hot tub before he passes out. I noticed at the Halloween party that it was out of service, and the first night of November is a cold one. Frost is already creeping across the grass. No one should bother us out here tonight.

I go back to my car and park it somewhere less conspicuous—out front on the same block as the SigUp house. Then I sneak through the gate again with supplies:

Spray paint.

An air horn.

His phone.

And a few dildos.

Tomorrow morning, there will be some very interesting photos of Charles sent to all his closest friends. Sent, of course, from his very own phone.

I take off his clothes. Then I use the spray paint to write RAPIST on his naked body—front and back—in a bright,

bright blue. Then, for extra fun, I spray his entire face and hair the same color. He should have a good time getting that out.

I start taking pictures. It's actually kind of fun positioning him in lots of embarrassing ways. The only flaw in my plan is not being able to see his face when he realizes what's happened.

When I'm finished, I check my watch. It's just past two. The lights in the house are off and it looks like all the brothers are sleeping soundly. Which makes what I'm about to do a little mean. I like most of the SigUp brothers. But Blake has to see my message. He has to know what really happened.

I position his body just the way I want it and take one last picture. Then I gather the rest of my things. It's almost time to do it.

I set up the air horn against some bricks so it will keep blasting long after I trigger it. As I place the last brick, its edge depresses the button on the horn. The sound is so loud it's jarring. I fly back, land on my ass. Scramble up again.

My ears are ringing and I want it to stop, but I have to get out of here. Lights have already started to flash on behind windows. I have to run.

I make it out the back gate just as I hear the back door open. There are a thunder of footsteps and then, mercifully, the horn stops. I stay quiet on the other side of the fence, not quite able to go away before I know they've seen him.

"What the fuck?"

"Who is that?"

"Is that a fucking dick in his ass?"

"No man, I think it's a dildo."

"Is he breathing?"

"I think so. But he's fucking wasted."

Then his voice. Blake's! "Jesus fucking Christ. Get him the fuck inside before we all freeze to death."

"What do you want me to do with this?" someone asks. I think it's Tucker.

"Pull it out, you dumb fuck," Blake says.

I can't help but to smile.

40

THE NEXT DAY, I SIT through class, listening to people gossip about all the pictures of Charles. He hasn't shown his face anywhere today. I imagine he's too embarrassed to show up looking like a cartoon character. Either that or he's still having a hard time sitting down.

I wait for a message from Blake all day, but nothing comes. Instead of studying during my last class, I write him another letter.

Dear Blake,

Oh, my Darling! Being away from you is murder. Absolute torture! I can't bear it much longer. I really can't.

You are my gasoline, my calories, my water, my life-giving energy source. Without you, I will die. Surely you've had time to think things over, haven't you? To see what really happened at the party?

I thought I took care of it. I thought that's what you'd want me to do. But still you refuse to tell me what I must do to make things right?

How are we supposed to build our relationship if you won't communicate with me? It's not possible. You have to stop the silent treatment before it's too late.

It was a drunken night, one drunken night. And you're the one who wanted me to drink, weren't you? Maybe you're looking for someone stronger, someone who can just drink anything and not feel it. Well, I think that's silly. I know, for a fact, Amber is a lightweight. So what's really going on here? Are you trying to send me a message? Was the other night a punishment? Just tell me so we can get past this hurdle in our relationship.

And besides, what am I supposed to think? You, out there running around with my sworn enemy. How do you think that makes me feel? Like shit, that's what.

Like total shit.

And that came first, my love. That came first.

I think maybe I understand. At least a little? Maybe you wanted him to care for me that night while you were stuck with her. Well, I'll tell you something, Blake Abbott. There is no substitution for you. Absolutely none. All other men are pitiful by comparison. Don't you dare think they can replace you. They can't. Don't feel that way, okay? Never, never again will I allow anyone to try.

Enclosed is a locket of my hair, burned from the back of my scalp. The pain is worth it if you come back to me. Send me yours? Please? Or anything. A sign. Something. A phone call?

I'm dying without you.

Your Darling

I shove it into the SigUp mailbox. But that night when I fall asleep, I still haven't heard from him.

One day a couple weeks after the Halloween party, Amber

comes home. She looks upset. She smashes things around in her closet, making such a clatter that it's clear she won't stop until I ask her what's going on.

"What's the matter?" I say.

"Ugh! Men!"

She's complaining about Blake right now, actually complaining about the most incredible person on the planet? Fuck her. I mean, really, fuck her.

Then I realize this could be good. This could be the perfect solution to all our problems. If she leaves Blake, then he has no obligations to her anymore, and she could hardly complain when we fall in love. And so what if she did? She would have been the one to dump him.

"What happened?"

"Oh, nothing," she says. She's taking off her clothes, looking for something else to wear. She must be between sorority events and in a hurry. Maybe she doesn't have time, but I need to get her talking. The more you talk about something, the more real it is. I need to get her boiling.

"It doesn't seem like nothing," I say.

"He's just really, really pissing me off. It's not a big deal."

"What did he do?"

She's flipping through her closet, hard, every hanger slapping against its neighbor as it lands.

"He got all mad because I was talking to some other guys at this little barbecue for the entire Greek community. It was stupid. I have to talk to everyone. It's part of being a good host. He knows that. And plus, I'm not officially inducted yet, so I have to do what my sisters say. And they specifically told us to make the rounds, don't stay in one place or talk to one person for too long. I had to. It wasn't like I was ignoring him. And it's not even like we said we'd be exclusive or anything. He just assumes we are, but I certainly never said that."

She was ignoring him, putting her loyalties to the sorority over her loyalties to him. I mean, what's really important here? I would have felt exactly the same way if I were Blake. Exactly the same.

She stops flipping through her closet. "You haven't seen my blue dress have you?"

"No, sorry. Have you checked your laundry basket?"

"Hmm, no. But I haven't worn it since that awful night we tried to hit all those parties and failed miserably. I could swear I washed it after that."

"So what made you think he was so mad?"

"Because he told me," she turns to me. "Actually, he said, and I quote, 'You need to be aware of how your actions reflect on me. How would it make you look if I left you alone at one of my parties?' He actually said that! Like the big deal wasn't that he wanted to be around *me* more, but that he didn't like the way it made *him look*! I mean, I knew he was a little bit of the jealous type, but this was in a whole other league. It just really made me see him in a new light, you know?"

I nod my head to keep her going.

"Honestly, I'm not even sure I want to be in a

relationship right now. Much less with someone who expects me to be his arm candy at all times. It's not worth it. It's really not."

"It doesn't sound like it."

"I mean, there were so many cute boys at that thing. So many."

Cuter than Blake? Not possible. But I imagine myself a fan; I imagine her a flame.

"They seem to be everywhere around here," I say.

"I know, right? It's like this place breeds them. It's crazy. And I didn't come to college to get tied down to one person. Especially not right now. I mean, I'm only a freshman."

"Then maybe you shouldn't be tied down."

"You know what, Greta? I think you're right. I think you're exactly right."

41

AFTER SHE LEAVES, I JUMP up and down. I actually jump. She's going to leave him! She's going to leave him! Blake was right to wait for things to work themselves out. He probably said all that stuff to make her angry, was probably glad she was ignoring him all night. It's perfect. It's absolutely perfect.

I shower and do my makeup and twist my hair into a high bun. I put on my highest heels and borrow a little black dress from Amber. Tonight is the night. We can finally be together.

I get to Blake's block around midnight. I'm just in time to see a group of guys, Blake included, walk out of the house together. They're laughing, dressed in black, and loaded down with ropes and backpacks. He looks like he's having fun with his guy friends. I don't want to interrupt him. I want tonight to be special. Maybe it's not a good time.

I decide to follow them instead. Maybe an opportunity will present itself and I'll jump out and surprise him. And this way I'll definitely be there when he's finished having boy time.

My black dress is perfect for sneaking through the shadows and the guys are so loud they don't notice me at all anyway. I could probably shout at the top of my lungs and they'd have no idea I was here. It's nice to see Blake having so much fun. He probably feels so relieved things with Amber are over.

As we round the next block, they guys get quiet. They stop at the corner and send a couple people ahead, who are crouched down and creeping toward a house in the middle of the block. I cross to the other side of the street so I can get a better view. It's another frat house. I don't know which one, but it's not SigUp. So why are these guys here?

The scouts come back and they whisper something to each other, then the whole group creeps over to the frat house. Then all of a sudden they're hoisting a guy up toward the portico that covers the front door. Then the guy is climbing up on the roof.

What are they doing? I wish I could hear what they're saying to each other. It's driving me mad.

I decide to walk down the block, across the street from them so I can get a little bit closer.

The guy on the portico is prying off one of their house letters, a big Greek Z, and two other Greek characters I can't identify. It must be a prank. Probably a rivalry between the two houses. How funny! I hope Blake wins!

Then a light flips on in a window right above where the

guy is standing. He yanks hard against the letter, so hard he loses his balance and almost falls off. But the letter comes free. Then there's a face at the window. Not a boy's face like I expected. A girl's. She swings the window open. It's Amber.

And she's only wearing her underwear.

She looks down and sees what's happening right away.

"Cam! Cam!" she's shouting, for something or maybe someone. I don't know which. She's looking over her shoulder back into the room. A man comes up behind Amber in the window. He's blond and tan and not wearing a shirt.

I guess Amber doesn't waste any time.

"Go, go, go!" the guy on the portico shouts. He tosses the letter down, then jumps right off the roof and tumbles onto the grass.

The other guys sprint off with the letters, but Blake stays put. He's staring up at her, his face confused, hurt, crushed even. Why would he feel that way?

Did she not end it? Did she just go out and cheat on him like a fucking whore?

I knew she was selfish, but this seems beyond even her.

"Shit," Amber says. "Shit." She scrambles away from the window and disappears into the space behind the guy.

"Stay there. Stay right fucking there, asshole," the guy says, then races away from the window.

Blake bolts off, looking for a place to hide. He needs me. I have to save him.

"Blake!" I scream, "over here!"

He whips his head around and sees me there, behind the bush.

"What the—?"

I wave him over. He seems indecisive for a moment, not sure if his best bet is to run or hide with me. But the streets are long and there's no way he'll get out of sight now before that guy makes it downstairs. He runs toward me. My heart leaps in my chest.

He barely gets inside with me when a horde of guys comes racing out. They split up and go in opposite directions. But Blake is safe. Blake is safe with me. *Because* of me.

He doesn't ask what I'm doing here. He knows.

"Are you okay?" I ask when they're gone.

"Yeah, thanks."

"I mean about Amber."

His face gets hard, annoyed even. "Amber? Why would I be upset about Amber?"

"Wasn't she with another guy up there?"

"Why would I care who she's with? I broke up with her at lunch today." This can't quite be true because Amber and I were talking only a couple hours ago, but I don't say anything. It's better for men if they have their pride.

Then I realize it actually could be true. Maybe Amber was lying to me. It wouldn't be the first time. It's either that or she was too stupid to understand *he* was breaking up with *her*.

"I know I'm supposed to say I'm sorry about Amber, but I'm not sorry," I say.

I kiss him, my lips meeting his under the moonlight winking through the branches. He pulls away at first, surprised by me, by my boldness. I like surprising him.

Then he grabs my face and smashes my mouth against his.

"You want me, don't you? You fucking want me."

"Yes," I say. Was this the trouble all along? Was he unsure of my devotion? "Of course I want you. Of course I do."

Before I know what's happening, I'm on the ground and my panties are off. He's flipping me over, holding me down, behind me, grinding into me, our desire exploding between us, fusing us together.

There are pine needles piercing my hands and my cheeks and pine cones tangling my hair but I don't care. All I see is him, all I feel is him, and this moment, with all its imperfections, is perfect.

We've wanted each other for so long it takes almost no time for us both to explode. I can't contain the surge that flows through my body. It erupts around me, envelops us both, and I feel his tremors too, the two of us joined in the moonlight.

He rolls off of me, panting, out of breath. He sits up, but I can't. I'm bowled over by the force of what just happened between us. I close my eyes and inhale the deep scent of the earth to remember this moment forever. This first, most perfect moment. The start of us.

When I turn over and open my eyes, he's standing up, buckling his belt.

"I have to go," he says. "I have to get back before they do something stupid."

Don't go, I want to scream. Stay with me here. All night. Forever. Don't go.

But a little voice inside reminds me that you have to let boys come to you. You have to play hard to get. Otherwise, he might not want to do it again.

I say nothing.

He reads the disappointment on my face. "You'll be fine, though, right?"

"Sure." Of course I will. Nothing could ever be wrong again.

He runs and runs and I can't catch up.

42

I KEEP RUNNING, THOUGH. ALL the way back to his house. After he gets home and sorts everything out, he will take me up to his bed and claim me as his own again. I will wait all night if I need to. I will wait all year.

But when I reach the Sigma Phi Upsilon house, there's crazy happening all over the front lawn. Boys brawling with boys. SigUp boys and the boys from the other frat. I think it must be Zeta-something because one of the letters from their house—the big Greek Z—is lying on the ground, the very last of the letters not smashed to pieces.

And right in the center of it all is my Blake, pounding on the boy from the window—Cam or whoever—the one who was with Amber. His face is bloody and raw. How cute is he now, Amber? Worth all the trouble? Not likely, you little slut.

Whoever he is, he's no match for Blake. Cam's body has gone wobbly, his eyes barely open. Blake rears back to hit him again, but his fist is stopped midair by Tucker and a few other SigUp brothers. It takes four of them to hold Blake back.

"Come on, man," Tucker says to Blake. "You got him, okay?"

Blake spits on the guy, and the glob lands on his swollen eye, slides down, clearing the blood to make a clean streak.

Then there is Amber screaming at everyone. Amber from where, I don't know. Has she been here the whole time? Did she see me? I want her to, but she's not looking at me. She's across the street. She's looking at Blake.

"What the fuck are you doing?" she asks, her sweet twang not sounding so sweet anymore. "Leave him alone."

Blake breaks away from the guys, stomps toward her. She takes a few steps back, scared of his mass, of the look in his eyes. She should be.

"The other girls told me, but I didn't believe them," she says. "I didn't believe you could be like this."

"What the fuck are you even doing here?" Blake asks. "Fucking slut."

Yes, Blake, yes. Finally.

"We weren't exclusive. You knew that."

"You don't get to tell me what to do, cunt. Get the fuck off my property. I could smell your rotten pussy from down the block."

The smile on my face, you wouldn't believe it. I just … I just can't explain how good it feels for him to finally see her as she really is.

"Jesus Christ," she says, eyes rolling, arms crossed,

growing taller. "You think saying somethin' stupid like that is gonna make you look better? Everyone can see what happened here. You got your little feelings hurt and this is what you did. You fucking fell apart." She huffs, then says, "What a joke."

She turns and walks away from him, but he lunges at her, knocks her to the ground, holds her down.

I want to shout at Blake to hit her.

Hit her!

Hit her!

Hit her!

But Tucker is on him immediately, so fast I didn't even see him move. Then other guys too, pulling him off. Guys from both houses—the fight suddenly stopped in favor of stopping this.

"What the fuck, man? She's a lady," a Zeta guy says.

"Leave it, man," a SigUp guy says.

"She's not worth it, bro," another guy says.

When they finally pull him off her, her hair is a rat's nest and she's crying up a storm of thick, fat tears down her makeup-smudged face. I almost have pity for her. Almost. But it's not like he even hurt her. She's crying over nothing.

A few guys get her to her feet, put distance between her and Blake. They walk her away, arms around her, rubbing her back like she's some fucking wounded bird instead of the lying, unfaithful whore she is.

Then there are police lights and people running and the Zeta's dragging Cam with them, down the street, into the darkness.

And Blake, just Blake, standing on the lawn staring across the street at me.

I take a step forward, my heart thrumming, my eyes wide with hope.

He walks inside the house and closes the door.

She really messed him up. She really did. And she'll pay for it.

Part Seven

My Johnny

43

IT TAKES ME MONTHS, LITERALLY months, of watching and waiting, to come up with a plan, one so great there's no way he could say no to me. By January, my grades are suffering, but it doesn't matter. I've already put in my application at lots of schools, including all the schools with major film programs. That way we can be together whenever he tells me which school he picked. I have a 4.0 GPA, and my SAT's are through the roof, so I have high hopes it will work out. And if I slip up a little bit now, no one will even notice. The schools already have my transcripts and I can make the grades up later.

It's hard to watch him without being noticed, but I've figured out some tricks. Because I have to see him. I must be with him.

The first thing I do is set up a fake profile on Facebook. There's a girl at our school who isn't on Facebook. I don't think she's allowed online at all because she's religious. She's really quiet and doesn't talk to people much, so I doubt anyone's noticed. I scan the picture of her from last year's yearbook and set up a profile like I'm her. I make sure to put lots of stuff on there about Jesus to make it look real. Johnny accepts my friend request right away, and now I can see what's going on in his life just by getting on my computer.

The next thing I do is drop Advanced Placement English at the end of first semester so I can transfer into his Intermediate English class. I tell the counselor the workload is just too much for me, which she seems to understand, even though I have the highest grade in the class. I've learned most people are much stupider than you give them credit for.

I keep my distance from him, sitting in the very back of class so I can watch him. I don't want him to know what I'm up to. I want him to be totally surprised. I think he will be.

What's harder are the times he's not in class. When he's at play rehearsals and basketball practice and eating breakfast in the morning and going out on the weekends. Those times are a challenge. I have to find places to hide where he won't even notice I'm there. It's like I'm his own private cheerleader.

It's not always easy. The dates with THAT GIRL are the hardest, but for a different reason.

Eventually, I start to learn his rhythms and habits. He sleeps in as late as he can every morning and his bed is a little too small for his lanky frame. He's probably had that old bed since he was a kid.

He wakes up in the morning sprawled across it, hanging off in some places, barely covered by the blankets, his temperature must run hot when he sleeps. His room is on the top floor of the house, but there's a hill behind it where, with binoculars, you can see right inside. He leaves the curtains open for me.

He always takes his skateboard to school on sunny days, even though he has a nice car his parents bought him for his sixteenth birthday. He stays up really late every night, sometimes until 2 AM, even on a school night. At basketball practice, he puts everything he can into the game. By the end, he's already worn out, but even then he doesn't give up. His sweat smells like the earth and he wears Fresh Breeze deodorant.

There are forget-me-nots planted in his backyard—a whole carpet of dainty blue flowers—up against the fence and behind the latch that you can't open from the outside but have to hoist yourself over. One day he will make me a bouquet of them to tell me he will never, ever forget me.

He likes sugary cereals, Captain Crunch and Fruity Pebbles, but Cocoa Puffs is his favorite. I ask my mom to buy some for us but she tells me it's a waste of money and if I want it I have to buy it myself. Instead, I just take a box from the gas station and hide it under a tarp in the back room. I imagine when I'm eating it that his kisses taste like sugar. It's too adorable to imagine without getting a big grin on my face.

What I'm looking for in all of this is an opportunity. I need to plan ahead to make sure it's exactly right. Nothing can go wrong. It has to be the perfect moment.

I finally get my chance in February. On Thursday night, I watch from under the trampoline in his backyard as his parents carry suitcases into the kitchen and kiss him goodbye. I don't know how long they'll be gone, but the suitcases must mean more than one day.

This is it.

I pretend I'm sick and skip school Friday. My mother is a germophobe so I know this will guarantee she leaves me alone and warns my dad to do the same. As soon as they leave for the gas station, I run a hot bath and fill it with a bottle of perfume I bought especially for this. I wash my hair and shave my legs and spread lotion everywhere.

When I'm done, there's not even a trace of the gas station on me. The perfume has soaked into my skin and made me smell like peaches and cream and cinnamon. Lots and lots of cinnamon.

I take out the curler set and wrap my hair in rollers, around and around and around, so many times it spills off the edges before I'm done. Then I sit under the old-fashioned hair dryer we got after my grandma died. It makes me feel like a fine lady, and I pretend I'm in the 1950's and having my weekly beauty parlor appointment so that when Johnny comes home I will look absolutely perfect.

While my hair is drying, I paint my fingers and my toes with a brand new bottle of nail polish: bright, ruby red. Then I put on lipstick to match. I have a little trouble putting it on and have to try a few times before it's just right. Who knew lipstick took so much practice? Where it went on wrong, there's just the hint of a red stain around my lips that won't come off, but it doesn't matter. It will be dark in there.

My hair unspools into long, glorious curls that cascade down my back and tame my natural frizz into a lovely mane. I look in the mirror, primed and polished and perfect. I am Venus emerging from the sea, born anew and ready for love. Tonight is the night. Tonight I will offer myself to Johnny.

It's too cold outside to leave the window open, so I'll have to leave before my parents get back and sneak in the back door afterward. I stuff pillows under my blankets in the shape of my body. I even managed to find a wig at the thrift store to peek out of the top of the covers. My parents always go to Frank's Bar on Friday nights, so I know they won't be home until late. They'll probably just open the door, see I'm sleeping and go to bed. But even if they don't, I don't care. All the punishments in the world wouldn't matter as long as I get tonight.

I take my new bike, which my parents made me buy with my own money once they saw what happened to the other one. They say taking responsibility for my things builds character, but I know they're just cheap. It takes a little longer to get there because I have to go the long way to avoid the gas station. But my new bike is faster than the last one and there's no traffic right now. School isn't even out yet, which is lucky because I want to surprise him.

44

I PICK A FLOWER FROM the garden, a forget-me-not, and tuck it behind my ear as I walk to his back door.

It's locked, which I knew it would be, but they never lock the deadbolt. There's a small piece of sheet metal in my backpack, a little smaller than a piece of bread and thin as a credit card. I got it out of my dad's tool shed just for this purpose. I slide the small square under the rubber casing and curve it until it tucks into the doorjamb. I wiggle it down toward the doorknob, pressing gently on the door at the same time. It pushes right open and I'm inside his house, as easy as that.

I hear the beep before I see it, but I'm prepared. It's coming from the kitchen, from beside the door that leads to their garage. I flip up the top of the security system keypad and enter the numbers I've watched them enter a hundred times: 4-8-8-5.

Only it doesn't stop beeping.

I enter it again, slowly, just to be sure I didn't do it wrong:

4-8-8-5.

Still, the beeping continues.

How is that possible? It's been the same code for months. I saw his parents enter it on the keypad before they left yesterday. Could they have changed it? Could I have seen it wrong?

My heart races and my breathing gets thin. How long has it been since I opened the door? Twenty seconds? Thirty? How long until the police are called automatically? Sixty seconds, I think. Sixty seconds and I'm already through half of them, maybe more.

I take a deep breath, try to think. I look at the wear patterns on the keypad, but it is clean of finger smudges. I look at the whiteboard on the wall and scan it for any numbers that might be a clue. But there's nothing that stands out. Just family notes and pictures and basketball practice times for the week.

Next to the whiteboard is a calendar. I flip through it to see if there are any Post-its labeled with the code. There aren't. There's practically nothing listed on it except for holidays and birthdays.

Then something clicks. I did see it wrong. It's not 4-8-8-5. It's 4-8-9-5. April 8th, 1995. Johnny's birthday. Of course it is.

I scramble back to the pad and punch in the numbers so hard it hurts my finger. 4-8-9-5.

The beeping stops.

The flashing red light turns to solid green and the

ARMED alert on the screen turns to DISARMED. I'm in.

I take a moment to soak it all in. I'm in his house. Finally. I've seen it, of course, but things are different from a distance: colder, and more reserved. Inside, this house has life and color and warmth. I let myself wander through the rooms, taking mental notes so I can recreate the same feel when Johnny and I move in together. He'll want things a certain way, I'm sure.

This house is much nicer than ours. It sits on a golf course, one of the few neighborhoods in Prairie Grove that was built in this decade. It's made for people who have good city jobs but want plenty of land to call their own and don't mind driving out of their way every day to get it. People exactly like Johnny's parents.

The rooms are wide and open with tall ceilings and fresh paint. There is new furniture everywhere instead of age-old hand-me-downs barely holding themselves together. The curtains match the accent pillows, which match the rugs. And the rugs themselves are strewn at just the right angle along the gleaming hardwoods to give it a relaxed feel. It's something so effortless-looking that it must have taken hours to perfect, like tousled hair or that pair of jeans that's dyed to look dirty. It works. The house feels comfortable—homey and new at the same time.

And everything is so clean! Where there are dust or spider webs in my house, the surfaces are clear and spotless. The countertops are shiny, some kind of stone I think, because they feel cold when I slide my hand across their smooth surface. Every appliance in the kitchen is stainless steel, from the refrigerator to the espresso machine. They even have a little, separate refrigerator just for wine.

"Would you like an espresso this morning, my darling?" I ask no one.

"Oh my love, you're so good to me," I answer back in my best impression of Johnny's voice. It makes me giggle.

I click on the machine and hear it whir and hiss. There's a bubbling sound and before I know it, the little spout bubbles out dark liquid. I scramble toward the cupboards for a mug and find them right away. They're exactly where they're supposed to be, directly above the machine. I feel right at home. This is where I belong. Not in some dilapidated farmhouse in the middle of nowhere.

I suck down my coffee and wipe up the bit that spilled with paper towels. When I place the mug in the dishwasher, I see the CLEAN light is on. I busy myself putting them all away, easily finding where things go because every piece is part of a matching set. Won't Johnny be so impressed with me?

Next, I walk upstairs, admiring the family photos on the wall as I go up. We've never had a family photo except for that time Aunt Peggy visited and made us pose out in front of the house. She sent us a print, but my mom stuffed it in a drawer somewhere rather than frame it.

These photos all look recent. They must have been taken this year. They're all in black and white with clean white mattes in clean white frames and were clearly done by a professional. The family must have gone to a park and did every pose possible because there's one of every combination of the four of them. One of his little sister Grace alone—her braces dominating the smile on her otherwise pretty fourteen-year-old face. One of Grace and Johnny together (he's such a good big brother, you can tell!) One of the whole family together, Johnny smiling with Grace between their parents.

There's even one of his parents together. They look so in love! I read somewhere that men with parents who really, truly love each other are far more likely to be faithful to their wives as adults. This picture gives me a lot of hope that what he's going through right now with *that girl* is only a phase. I almost love the picture of his parents the most. Almost.

Right at the top of the stairs is the one I really love. It's of Johnny by himself. He's sitting on the ground with his back against a tree. His hands are relaxed on his knees, which are propped up and spread in a wide stance. But the best part is his face. He's not smiling into the camera like our lame school photos. He's not being model-serious either, like some of the boys at school do in their senior pictures. He's laughing. His head tilts back so far that his Adam's apple stick's out against the strong tendons in his neck. His face is catching a spot of sunshine and crinkled in full-throttle joy. I've never seen him happier. I imagine myself sitting between those legs and his arms tight around me. I can almost feel them. I lean forward and kiss his mouth, leaving lipstick lips on the glass. It will be his only clue. Aren't I sneaky?

I make my way through all the bedrooms, laying on every bed like Goldilocks. There's a bathroom attached to his parents' bedroom that's bigger than any bathroom I've ever seen except on the movies and just as luxurious. I sniff at his mother's perfume and check my reflection in the mirror. I look perfect. Wild and alive and ravishing. My long hair curls down my body like Rapunzel. The only thing that's not working is my outfit, which is old and stained in places. I take it off and look again at my naked body in the mirror. That's better.

For a moment, I debate the idea of his parents' bedroom as the place but decide against it. Instead, I go to his room and make the bed. It feels kinky to be making his bed in the nude. I imagine him watching me from the corner as I tuck the sheets and fluff his pillow, bent over so he can see everything.

I lay down on top of the covers and arrange my hair just so. I imagine I am the Lady of Shalott and his bed is my boat. I close my eyes and pretend I am dead. Eventually, I drift off to sleep.

45

A NOISE STARTLES ME AWAKE. The slam of a door downstairs, the flutter of feet. And voices, which is wrong somehow. Grace is on a class trip to the mountains and shouldn't be home until Monday. I'm probably hearing things. Then the voices get louder and I realize it's the TV. I had hoped he'd come straight to his room. It's okay. I can be patient.

I listen, trying to guess what he's watching, but I can't place it. Some art movie probably. He's probably studying his craft in his free time. It's sweet, but he'll regret wasting time on it instead of me very soon. There's a grin plastered on my face and my heart is racing. The temptation to walk down the stairs and surprise him is overwhelming. But I've imagined this moment so many times and I want it to be just perfect. He needs to see me here, in his bed. His. All his.

After what feels like forever, the movie turns to music. At first I don't realize it. I think it's just a commercial or that he's watching music videos or something. But minutes of songs go by without discernible voices in between. I check the clock and see it's 6:45 PM. I wonder what he's doing down there?

For a moment, I wish I were on the hill with my binoculars so I could see him. Is he cooking? Dancing? Playing video games without the sound? I try to imagine him dancing, but can't. Not without me at least. He must be making dinner, but I don't smell anything.

I'm starting to get cold. I want to tuck in under the covers, but the image of me would be totally ruined. I let the bumps rise on my skin and imagine his heat making them disappear. Why won't he just get up here already?

There's a loud chime. A doorbell? The door slams again and there are new voices. Lots of them. Then more chimes and more voices and suddenly I'm scared. What's going on?

The music gets turned up loud and I realize exactly what's happening. He's having a party. Of course he is. His parents are gone for the weekend. Why didn't I consider this? Why didn't I go to school today or check Facebook this morning? There was probably an invitation there, or a comment or some hint this would be happening tonight.

I don't know what to do. My moment is ruined. Other people were never part of the plan. I try to think of ways to escape without anyone seeing me, but there's only one way out and that's down the stairs. Besides that, my clothes are lying on the floor in his parent's bedroom across the hall. The hall itself is an open loft space that you can see from below. There's no way I could get them without being seen, and if I leave them behind, someone will find them. Probably him, and then he'll know. He won't be surprised and I'll have to come up with something entirely different to do instead.

This is awful. I wish I were dead. My heart pounds like crazy.

What do I do?

What do I do?

What do I do?

There's really only one option. I will wait. Eventually, people will leave and he'll stagger up the stairs to fall asleep in his own bed. And when he does, I'll be there waiting. Nothing has changed, not really. I close my eyes and take deep breaths to calm down.

This can still work.

This can still work.

This can still work.

I tiptoe over to the door and search the doorknob for a lock, but there isn't one. I lay back down on the bed, but feel exposed now instead of excited, weak and vulnerable instead of confident and alluring.

Then a terrible thought comes. What if somebody else comes in here and tries to do what I want only Johnny to do? What if Johnny sends someone up here as a final test of my loyalty? I need something to defend myself with. I scan the room for a weapon, but Johnny's not the kind of guy who carries a knife or goes out hunting on the weekends.

There's not even a baseball bat in here.

I reach out for a large metal "J" on his dresser, the decorative kind that's the size of a dictionary. It's heavy in my hands, as solid as an anchor. The cool smoothness of it calms me. I lie back down on the bed and set it on my chest. The weight of it forces me to slow my breath and still my fluttering heart. I watch the rise and fall of it there, and it feels just right—his first initial branded between my breasts. I watch it go up and down and up and down. And I wait.

The party roars below my feet. Music pounds and voices swell in laughter and shouts. I think they're probably drinking, which makes me disappointed in Johnny. When we're together, I'll make him stop.

He should really know better than to act like this. He should have felt me right away when he came home. Maybe he was too distracted by his plans for the night or too tired from a long day. But still, he should have known.

I feel myself getting angrier and angrier at him. I hate being angry at my Johnny. I hate it. Why would he do this to me? Test me like this? Keep me waiting when we both know the time has come to make peace with each other.

A knock on the door interrupts my thoughts.

"Hello?" It's a guy, but that voice is not Johnny's.

It's happening. Someone's trying to get me.

46

I GRAB THE J AND dive off the bed onto the floor, making a loud *thunk* as my body hits the carpet.

Another knock. A hard one this time. I get to my feet and crouch low, raising the J above my head, ready for him.

"Somebody in there?" he says. Then there's a noise I wasn't expecting. A girl giggles.

It doesn't make sense. Why would there be a girl?

"I think it's probably free," the girl says.

"I don't know. I thought I heard something." Another knock.

"Come on. Let's just go in. There's nobody in there."

"Last chance or we're coming in," the guy says, pounding at the door again like a machine gun.

This isn't a test. It isn't what I thought at all. It's just two kids who want to be alone.

I dive under the bed as fast as I can, burning my back and butt cheeks against the carpet as I wiggle under, the J still solidly in my grasp. There's barely enough room for me under here, under the square-woven bedsprings straining against the weight of the mattress. I make it under just in time.

The door opens. I see two sets of feet, but can't make out who they belong to. The guy is wearing tennis shoes and the girl is wearing the kind of shoes I heard someone at school call fuck-me-pumps because they're so high and make you look so slutty I guess. She kicks them off and lands on the bed, her bare feet dangling off the edge. I can see a tiny blister just starting to pop from the back of her heel.

"Get over here," she says.

There are wet smacking sounds and moaning and soon the guy's pants are down around his ankles and then completely off and the girl's bra is on the floor. They flop onto the bed and it bounces from their weight, sending the bedsprings hard against my breasts and my face. I have to bite my lip to stop myself from screaming as the bare wire nicks my skin. I want to turn over, but there's not enough space, less than a foot.

Then they laugh, and the bed stills as they whisper something to each other I cannot hear. I try to quiet my breathing, which has gotten too fast. It seems like they should be able to hear my thumping heart, but they can't, can they? No, they can't. They don't know anyone else in the world exists but themselves. It's exactly like that when I'm with Johnny.

The smacking sounds continue and I don't want to listen,

but I am listening and the sound of them together makes my body ache for Johnny. Harder, it feels, than I've ever ached before in my life. But he is not here, and it makes the hurt grow. These others are here and they are doing what we should be doing and I can't listen to them without crying.

"What was that?" the boy says.

"Huh?"

It's me, I realize. My little whimpers. I hold my breath, force myself to stop, feel the tickle of the snot as it dribbles out of my nose and onto my cheek. I don't dare move.

"I thought I heard something."

"It's nothing. You're being paranoid. Now get back here," the girl says. "I need you."

They're kissing again and it sounds wet and sloppy. I'm sickened by it and shove my fingers deep into my ears. They shouldn't be allowed to kiss. Not here. Not on the night he was supposed to be mine. Mine and Johnny's, not theirs.

All of a sudden the bed starts to bounce violently. The springs nick at my skin again and again and again. I yank my fingers out of my ears, trying to cover myself with my hands. But there's not enough of my hands to cover all the places where the metal scratches and pulls. It's pulling me apart.

The girl screams and she sounds like she's dying. I feel like I'm dying, and I scream too. Loud, loud, loud.

Make it stop.

Make it stop.

Make it stop.

"What the fuck?!" the boy says.

I'm screaming again. I can't stop screaming. The girl is screaming too, only it sounds different now, terrified. They know I'm here, and I don't care. I scream and scream and scream.

The boy hops off the bed and looks underneath, right at me. I know him. It's Duncan Taylor, the photographer for the school newspaper. Which means the girl will be Kristi Simms, *that girl's* best friend.

"Jesus Christ. Jesus Christ, there's somebody under there," Duncan says.

"What-the-fuck-what-the-Fuck-what-the-FUCK?" Kristi says.

I scramble out from under the bed, still clutching the J.

Kristi is standing on the bed tucked into the far corner near the headboard. She's clutching Johnny's blanket to cover her grotesque naked body and screams when she sees me. I snarl back, low and guttural and mean as a grizzly.

How dare they? In Johnny's bed. How DARE they?

Downstairs the music stops and there's a thunder of feet getting closer. Duncan, naked too, shifts to stand in front of Kristi. He holds his arms out as if I'm a soccer ball and she is the goal.

I feel something wet drip down my chest and realize it's blood. There are tiny cuts all over my body, dripping like a pincushion stigmata. I don't know what to do other than run.

The door flies open before I can get to it and *that girl* is in the doorway, Johnny right behind her.

"Kristi?!" Mindy says. She looks back and forth between them and me. I'm sobbing now instead of screaming.

"What's going on?" Johnny says. "Greta? What are you doing here?"

I fly toward him. All I want is to collapse into his arms. He will fix this. He will fix everything. But before I make it to him Mindy is between us, a wild look in her eye, pushing me away.

"No!" she says. Did she think I was going to hurt him? Did she actually think I could ever hurt the love of my life? My blood boils at the thought. She's done enough—too much. I should have put a stop to this a long time ago.

"I told you she was nuts," Mindy says to Johnny. "I told you she was going to freak out on you someday."

My arm moves independently of me. I see it curl in an arc above me as though in slow motion, though I put every ounce of strength I have into that throw.

The J twists through the air, head over heels, right toward her head. But before it can get there—before it can put an end to things—Johnny knocks Mindy to the side. It hits him instead, square in the forehead, with a chilling crack.

His face goes slack, his muscles too. He crumples to the ground, but I don't hear the thud above my scream. Blood trickles out from the spot where it made contact.

Someone's arms are on me, maybe more than one person. There is a sick feeling in my stomach and my legs lose their strength. I want to force them to stay upright, to take me to his side, but they refuse. My arms are rubber, useless. My bottom hits the person behind me, sending both of us to the floor with my dead weight. Everything goes dark. The last thing I see is Johnny's face.

When I regain consciousness, the police are swarming around me, and Johnny is being raced out of the room on a stretcher.

Part Eight

My Blake

47

I'M CLEANING UP. AMBER HAD to leave lab early. Again. More stupid Kappa stuff.

I'm the last one here. This was a rough one, electrophoresis, and I really could have used her help. But whatever. After what she did to Blake, I'd rather do the lab myself. I'm putting the dyes back in the cabinet: Bromophenol Blue, Orange G, Cibacron Blue, Xylene Cyanole. I put the last one in, Phenol Red, and I see him out of the corner of my eye.

It feels like my heart will explode.

"Hi," he says.

"You came." I can feel every muscle in my body trembling like I'm riding my bike down a gravel road.

He's here.

He's actually here.

"I did."

We end up at an old Dairy Queen off Dunberry Road. It smells like cows out here, but it's quiet enough to talk, far enough away that most students don't venture out. We sit at a cracked plastic table, once a vibrant red but now faded to pink from years in the harsh sun. He's stabbing his spoon at a banana split with extra strawberry. My hot fudge sundae has gone all soupy. Flies kamikaze themselves to steal a sugar buzz.

"It was for the best, you know?" he says.

"Do you really mean that?"

"Absolutely."

We're sitting together, having ice cream. Everyone who drives by will know we're on a date. A real, actual date.

"She's an amazing person, she really is, but girls like her? I don't think they want the same things I do. They're not serious, you know? It's all about parties and looking hot and hooking up."

"Exactly," I say.

"It's my own fault. I'm always falling for girls like that."

"Like Jessica too?"

"Yes. But not anymore. I want to be with someone real. Someone passionate. Someone who actually gives a shit about me."

He puts his hand on my hand, and I go all stiff—like I'm a cardboard cutout of myself instead of a real person.

"Call it a resolution," he says, then he grabs my face in his hands and kisses me. He tastes like raindrops and sunshine and smells like new leather and spices.

I kiss him back with everything inside of me. We have so much lost time to make up for. My tongue delves into his mouth, searching and tasting. I want to get closer to him—so close—but the damn table is between us.

"Come on," he says. He tugs my hand and pulls me behind the store. There's a hill that drops down to a ravine back there, and we traipse down it, nearly tripping because it's so steep and we're going so fast. Eventually, we reach the water's edge. The place is covered in trees. All their leaves are either golden or red or already dropped to the ground—shed for the crisp winter air that blows through them even now.

Blake unzips my jacket and slips it off my shoulders as he backs me against a tree. Then he slides his cold hands under my shirt. Goose pimples dot my skin, but the sensation is amazing. My nipples go stiff under his pinching fingers. And he's pinching me so hard it almost hurts. But the pain is good somehow, better than without it. I moan. The sound of it echoes off the trees.

In the next instant, he's pulled my shirt and my bra over my head, using them to cinch my wrists together. He holds them up against the tree with one hand and leans down to suck my nipples as his other hand roams into my jeans and icy bark presses into my back.

This is exactly what I want from him. Exactly what I've always wanted.

The wind whips by and the chill of it is almost unbearable. If it weren't for his hands on me, his mouth, I would freeze.

He unbuttons my jeans and slides them down my hips,

kissing my belly as he does so. Then my panties follow.

"Bend over and put your hands on the tree," he says.

I obey.

He must like looking at the back of me. This is almost the same as it was the first time we made love. It must be his favorite view.

I listen, bent over like that, as he unbuckles his belt and lets his pants drop to the forest floor. Then he pushes into me without warning. I gasp, shocked, sharp pain exploding inside of me.

It's different this time—a different place than before, even more intimate—and it hurts as much as it feels good, maybe more. Wild sensations are flooding over me, fast and raw and I can barely keep myself still long enough for him to keep finding me again and again and again.

He pumps fast and hard, owning me more deeply with every thrust. Soon the cold is gone, replaced by a hot rush all over my skin. The pain is gone too. I've accepted him, opened to him fully. And now there is only pleasure.

Too fast I hear him grunting behind me, pressing into me deep as his body spasms against me.

I did this. I made him do this, feel this way. I've never felt a greater satisfaction in my life.

He buckles up, and it doesn't matter that I still ache for him, that the spot between my thighs is flexed tight and still ready. After this, I can't imagine the feeling will ever go away. I'll hold on to it, let my aching need remind me of him with every step I take. There will be plenty of time for my own satisfaction later.

We have our whole lives ahead of us.

48

BACK IN THE CAR, I reach for Blake's hand as he drives me toward my dorm.

"How do you want to handle things with Amber?" he asks.

"What do you mean?" I ask. I can't wait to tell her. I can't wait to see the look on her stupid, prissy face.

"Well, I want her to know as soon as possible, of course," he says. "If I'm honest, I can't wait for her to see what it looks like when a woman actually pleases a man."

I pleased him. He said I pleased him. The place between my thighs still aches.

"Me too," I say, both relieved and excited that he wants to show the world as much as I do.

"My only concern is you," he says, squeezing my hand.

"You don't have to worry about me. I don't care what she thinks."

I watch the window fog from my breath as the trees whip past and snowflakes start to fall. It's the first snow of the year, and everything feels so peaceful, so right. It's almost like Blake and I made it happen, that we unleashed the snow with our love.

"It's not so much her as it is the rest of them," he says. "They're gong to say some pretty awful things, you know?" He looks over at me with concern etched in his features..

But this is something I've never considered. I've only ever thought about the two of us together. Not anyone else. No one else matters.

"Like what?" I ask.

"She's probably going to say you're a slut. That you were sleeping with me behind her back all along and that's why she cheated on me. It's kind of the perfect cover story if you think about it."

"But that's not even true!" I say, outraged.

"I know. But she's popular, and everyone loves to see someone as powerful as I am get tarnished. I don't care, of course. But the rumor will spread. Both of our reputations will suffer."

"That's so unfair."

"I know," he says. "But that's what'll happen. She'll use it to her advantage."

"Then we should wait to tell her," I say. The only thing that can't happen out of all of this is Amber winning—getting away with cheating on Blake. She doesn't deserve to win. She deserves to suffer.

"I don't know," he says. "Why should we hide? I refuse to be ashamed of how we feel about each other."

My heart sings at his words, but I won't let this destroy him. It's up to me to make sure it doesn't.

"No. Listen," I say. "All we have to do is wait a little while. If we give it a week or two, then no one would believe it."

"But I want to see you," he says, letting go of my hand so he can press it between my legs.

My breath nearly leaves me. I can't concentrate, can't think of anything but his hand, his hand, his *hand*.

"I want to show the world you're mine," he says, pressing even harder, rubbing me through my jeans.

He's pressing too hard now and I'm too close. I lose it. I can't help it. He already built me right to the edge and his hand just feels so good and I can't stop the rush of it when it comes.

I let out a long, wild groan, grabbing his hand and holding it to my crotch as my legs stretch in spasms and my head strains back against the seat.

"Fuck," I whimper. "*Fuck.*"

"Jesus fucking Christ," he says with a smirk, his hand still on the wheel. "That was easy."

He likes how he makes me feel. He likes to give me pleasure. He loves it.

"You like that?" he asks.

"Yeah," I say, my head finally starting to clear, my breath finally slowing back to normal.

"Me too," he says, his voice dropping low. "That's why I can't imagine not seeing you for a few weeks."

"You can still see me," I say, my mind made up now. I have to be the strong one, the smart one. "We'll find a way. And it's only for a little while. Just long enough to make sure she doesn't use it against us."

"Do you think that would really work?" he asks.

"It's the only way, Blake. We have to keep quiet. Just for a little while."

I sleep well that night, the best sleep I've ever had in my life. It's amazing what love will do to you.

In the dining hall at breakfast the next morning, I load my tray with waffles and bacon and eggs and a bowl of cereal too. I'm starving, ravenous, and eat until I can feel my belly protruding over my jeans. I don't care.

When I get back to the room, Amber is there with Claire—her sorority sister and the girl who said all those terrible things about my Blake. They're sitting on the bed together like lesbians. I want to slap Claire's face, but I decide to be the better person. Maybe Blake worked his magic on the Kappas. Maybe she's finally here to apologize.

Amber looks up at me with a worried expression and takes a deep breath. Claire gives her hand a little squeeze.

"I need to talk to you about something, Greta." It's then I notice there's a bag at her feet.

"Okay."

She reaches for her pillow and pulls the pillowcase off. Cat hair billows out and she coughs, tosses it to the side.

"You did this, didn't you?" Amber says.

"What are you talking about? What is that?"

"Don't lie, Greta! No one else comes in here. You're the only one who could have done it."

"You think I put cat hair in your pillow? Why would I do something like that? That's crazy."

"I don't know, but I found this too." She lifts up her blue dress, ripped from when I tore it off myself. "And then you were at that party on Halloween, spying on me and Blake and, and—" she looks to Claire for help.

"We found one of Amber's sweaters under the buffet table at the house," Claire says. "And somebody had peed on the carpet under there too. Did you break into our house?"

I don't say anything. Don't know what to say. If they've come to the point of putting these things together, there's nothing I can say. I just look at my hands. Blake was right. She's already trying to act against me.

"I didn't do those things," I say. "I really didn't."

"I thought we were friends, Greta. I really did."

"Well, we're not," I say. "Not anymore." For a split second, I almost consider telling her everything—that he's mine now, that he feels so amazing moving inside of me. But I hold my tongue. I won't let her use us to her advantage.

"I'm moving out, into the Kappa house. I was gonna do it soon anyway, but I'd feel better if we weren't living together anymore."

"Do whatever you want," I say. It's actually perfect. This

way Blake can see me more often, spend the night without her prying eyes around to see.

"I'll be around next weekend to pack up all my things," Amber says.

"Okay. Whatever."

She shakes her head. Claire says, "I think it would be best if you weren't around when we came. And I'm sure I don't have to say it, but if we see you lurking around anywhere near her again, we will call the police and report it to campus security."

"Oh, please," I say.

"This behavior isn't normal, Greta. It's scary. Maybe you should get some help. There's free counseling at the—"

"Help? You think I need help? Maybe take a look in the mirror you stupid, selfish cunts."

Amber huffs, speechless. The two of them stare at me and I glare back at them with fire in my eyes. I bet you didn't expect that, bitch, I want to say. I bet you didn't expect any of it.

"I don't get it," Amber says, tears cracking her voice. "I only ever tried to be nice to you." Her voice sounds like the whiniest, most pathetic voice I've ever heard in my life.

"Sure you did."

"I think we should go," Claire says.

Amber picks up her bag and Claire grabs her backpack. I can't wait for her to be gone. It had to happen. It did. It's better this way.

But before they go, Amber turns to me, wiping her eyes.

"Just tell me one thing. That night of the fire at the Tri-Alpha house? Who was the boy you were with?"

"None of your business," I say.

"That's what I thought," she says. "There was never a boy, was there?"

"Oh, there was a boy," I huff. If she only knew.

"Then let *him* cover for you," she says. "I'm going to the police and telling them I wasn't with you."

A vice tightens around my throat as I see her reach for the door. She can't do that. She can't.

"Amber, don't. Please. I didn't do anything. I swear.

"Goodbye, Greta," Amber says, and then she's gone.

49

HE KNOCKS AT MY DOOR at 6 PM. He looks exhausted from his day but has flowers and wine. I can't help but to beam. They are the first flowers anyone's ever bought me and they make me forget all about the nastiness with Amber today.

"Oh, my darling, they're beautiful," I say. "Thank you."

"No problem," he says, pecking me on the cheek. He looks around the room, a little put off, I think, by all Amber's junk. "You sure she's not going to be around tonight?"

"Of course not, silly. Tonight is just for us."

And it is. I can't deal with the Amber problem right now. Later, I'll figure out what to do to keep her quiet. And I will do something. I refuse to let her destroy my life, no matter what. But right now, I need *him*.

I kiss him again. For real this time.

"Make yourself comfortable," I say. He sits on my bed.

Blake. In my bed. It doesn't even seem real.

I don't have anything to put the flowers in, so I grab an old takeout cup and go down the hall to the bathroom to fill it with water. When I get back, he's done the sweetest thing. There's a picnic laid out on my desk. Wine in red solo cups, cheese, strawberries, candles. It's like a movie.

I've pinched myself before in dreams, actual dreams, and it never works to wake me. I go on sleeping, not realizing my experiences are an illusion. So I don't pinch myself this time. I just enjoy it.

"Is this okay?" he asks.

"Of course. It's more than okay. It's perfect."

"Good." And he smiles that perfect smile at me this time. "I thought we could watch a movie or something? It's been a long day. Sorry to be so lame."

"No. Don't apologize. I love movies," I say, excited. "And I have the perfect one."

I rummage in my closet for the DVD. It's been my favorite since I was a little girl. But now I have a prince, a handsome prince who has pulled me out of the depths and placed my feet on dry land. I hand it to him, my eyes bright and hopeful. I can't wait to share this with him.

"The Little Mermaid?" he asks. The expression on his face isn't what I thought it would be. I expected him to be moved, touched in fact. But he looks confused. Confused and not just a little bit amused.

"It's okay. We don't have to watch it," I say.

"No. It's fine. I just—" he pauses to take a deep breath. "I've never seen it before."

My face lights up. Of course! He couldn't possibly know why it's so special if he's never seen it.

"Never?" I ask. "That's crazy!"

"Nope."

I guess I still have a lot to learn about boys.

"Well, then we have to watch it. We absolutely have to. You're gonna love it."

The TV is Amber's, but she hasn't taken it away yet. I don't know what I'll do when she does. I'm completely out of money. I slide the disc in and the familiar music starts.

He sits on my bed with both of our drinks.

"To my first time watching the Little Mermaid," he says, raising his cup. We clink our glasses. At least in my mind it's a clink, really it's just a soft thud as the plastic of his cup meets mine.

"To us," I say and drink.

Then I snuggle up to him close, leaning my face into his chest. There's a perfect nook for me there, a dip under his shoulder that's the exact shape of my head. He drapes his arm around me and rubs my back, reaching down to lift up my shirt so he can make contact with my skin. Then he reaches around to grab my breast and squeezes it hard. The feel of it is electric.

I turn away from the TV to look up at him and he looks down at me and we kiss, right as Ariel is crooning "Part of Your World." Then his hand is pressing the top of my head down, down, down.

At first I don't get it.

"Come on, babe," he says. "Don't you want to make me happy?"

I think I understand, then. I think I know what he wants me to do. I've never done it before, but I overheard some girls talking about it in the locker room once. Then I looked it up online to be sure they weren't lying. But I can't believe it's something he wants *me* to do. His love feels like winning the lottery.

I wiggle down between his legs as he unzips his jeans. Then I put my lips around his hard cock. He's so big he barely fits in my mouth, and he moans as he slides past my lips. He must like that there's no extra space. I bob forward, but he flinches back, taking it away, pulling himself out of me.

"Teeth," he says. "Jesus."

"What?" I ask.

"Cover your fucking teeth," he says. "With your lips."

"Oh!" I say, understanding.

I hurt him. I hurt my love! My face flushes bright red. I'm so stupid. So fucking stupid.

"You're not gonna freak out on me, are you?" he asks.

"No," I say, only it sort of comes out like I already am freaking out.

"Come on," he says. "You already said you'd do it. Don't be a fucking tease."

"I'm not," I say, trying to get ahold of myself. He still wants me. That's what's important. He still wants me.

I try again. This time, I lick him all the way up and

down. Then I lick my lips and stretch them over my teeth before taking him all the way into my mouth.

"That's right," he says. "That's the way."

I'm doing it. I'm doing a good job.

Then his hand twists into my hair and he's pushing himself into me. The tip of his cock slams into the back of my throat, filling me up so much I can barely breathe, making my eyes water. He holds me there, thrusting into my mouth over and over, harder and harder, until the skin behind my lips is screaming. Until my teeth make tiny indentations in my own skin instead of his. Until I can taste my own blood.

"You like it when I fuck your mouth?" he asks.

I couldn't answer if I tried. All I can do is moan … moan *yes*.

Yes, I like it, I want to say. Of course I like being his. I fucking love it.

Then he's jerking inside me, and his spray hits the back of my throat, and my thighs are pressed together so tight I nearly come without him even touching me this time. When I finally taste air again, it is mingled with the taste of him and it's the sweetest thing I've ever breathed.

But he doesn't want me to have it for long. He flips me over, takes my jeans off, uses them to tie my wrists to the headboard.

"Spread yourself," he commands. "Come on, do it. Get me hard again."

I knew it was his favorite view.

I obey, letting my legs spread wide and tilting my pelvis so he can see every part of me. Behind me, I think he starts to touch himself.

It doesn't take long. I hear the rip of the foil, hear him slide the condom on, and then he's pushing into me. It only takes the one thrust for me to come apart. When I do, he presses my face into the pillow as my entire body shudders. And I can't tell if it's from the intensity of my pleasure, or from the lack of air, but my head gets suddenly hazy. I'm drifting in the clouds, swimming deep under the sea as he plunges into me over and over and over. Then everything goes dark.

50

I HAVE A FUZZY-HOT feeling in my mouth. My head is sludge and my thoughts are blurry—a little too blurry—images of things I can't quite make out, but know all the same. How much did I drink last night? I don't remember having more than a small glass of wine. But perhaps sleeping with him—finally sleeping next to him—has deepened my slumber. The sun finally pries my eyes open and the first thing I see are his eyes. They are warm, green with glints of gold, and they are staring right at me.

"Hey, gorgeous. How'd you sleep?"

There's a squeeze and I realize his arms are around me. I tilt my head and my cheek hits his chest. I inhale the skin and shale scent of him.

"Perfect. You?"

"Perfect," he says. He kisses me on the forehead, shifts.

"You okay?" I ask.

He takes a minute to register my words.

"I know it must be weird for you," I say. "To keep this

from everyone. So I don't think we should wait any longer. We'll tell her today, and then we'll tell everyone else. What do you think?"

"Sounds perfect," he says. Then he kisses me. "Why don't you come by my place later and we'll figure it all out?"

He rolls me on my back, kneeling over me, and I memorize the weight of him, part of me worrying it won't be there when I open my eyes—when I really wake up. His kiss is the kind you could disappear in.

He gets up. "I gotta get going. House meeting. They'll kill me if I miss another one."

I make a moany sound, a why-so-soon plea.

"But I'll call you later, okay?" he says, kissing me again. His kisses taste like thunder.

"Okay," I say, my tone whiny and pouting. I'd be perfectly happy to have him stay all day and into tonight and tomorrow and the next day and the next.

"Later then," he says, picking up something on his way to the door.

"What's that?" I ask.

He holds it up. My trash. He's taking out my trash. Could this boy be more amazing?

"Aren't you sweet?"

"I aim to please," he says, his hand on the doorknob.

I race over to him for one last kiss, but he turns away before my lips reach his.

"I really have to hurry, sorry." There's a little tremor in

his hand as I grab it. That's the kind of effect we have on each other.

"Don't make me suffer," I say, my head tilted back and my eyes closed.

And he doesn't make me suffer, not at all. He leans in and gives me the kind of kiss memories are made of, intense and hard and wanting. His hand clutches the back of my head, pulling my ponytail back and forcing my chest against him with a power I've never felt before. He kisses me so hard there might be bruises on my lips when he's done with me. I never want him to finish.

But eventually, he does.

"Bye," he says, with a cocky grin to tell me I belong to him.

"Bye," I say as he walks out the door.

I stretch, waking my limbs to the glorious day. I look over at Amber's bed, perfectly made, untouched last night as I knew it would be. She's going to take it so hard when we tell her. Sometimes you don't realize what you really have until you've lost it. Maybe it will finally teach her not to mess with me.

Then I remember something.

I take a moment to consider. She's not coming back for a few days still.

Carefully, even though I'm certain there's no danger in it because I've done it before, I reach up to the top shelf of her wardrobe. They're still there, shoved behind a winter coat it's not yet cold enough to use. The glasses, the ones

Blake should have given to me that night.

I put them on and look in the mirror. They're perfect. And they're mine.

She'll never miss them.

51

I WALK TO MY FIRST class, Calculus, like I'm walking on air, floaty and light.

All I can think about is Blake, so I decide to call him. It's what I can do now because I'm the new Amber. Me.

It's still hard to believe. I'd always hoped it would happen someday. I thought I was in love before, in high school, but this is different. This is better. With Johnny, I was happy, but with Blake I feel like I could fly. I feel like I could kiss the stars and rearrange them in the shape of his face.

I pull up his name on my phone, dial the number he put in himself. Himself! I get his voicemail, which is him laughing and then shouting his name, "BLAKE!" I feel like shouting mine back, to be funny, but I don't.

"It's me." Am I really saying that? "I just wanted to say hi. I'm glad it happened, you know? I really am. It's all going to work out. It has to. I love you." I do.

I-love-him-I-love-him-I-love-him-I-love-him! And he loves me too. It's the most amazing thing.

Blake will call me back soon and ask me over to his room. We will make love in the hazy afternoon, reaffirming the greatness that is us.

My path takes me through the academic courtyard, a big grassy space with lots of trees. Their leaves are drifting off, turning the crisp air into a fanfare of red and gold, like sparks from a sparkler.

As I'm getting close to the math & sciences building, I spot a huge commotion by the doors. Red and blue lights flash against yellow crime scene tape. There are officers in uniform and a white van that says "Mobile Forensics Lab" in big blue letters.

I get closer, but a crowd is starting to form and it's hard to see what's going on.

"What happened?" I whisper to another girl in the crowd.

She turns to me, her eyes alight with gossip, the kind that looks like fear on top of your face, but simmers with giddy excitement underneath.

"Somebody found a body in the Biology lab. A girl. A freshman."

"What?"

"I know. It's horrible, isn't it?" she says.

"Terrible."

"And she's a sorority girl. Apparently, she was wearing a Kappa T-shirt. That's what people are saying at least," she says.

A little hardness starts forming in my gut, like I just

swallowed a handful of pebbles.

"Do you know her name?" I say.

"Nobody knows. The police aren't saying anything."

"It wasn't a girl named Amber, was it?"

"I don't know. Sorry."

I walk away from her, wedging into the crowd closer and closer until I'm up against the police tape, until I'm breathing the exhaust of the idling ambulance to my right.

Then the police appear at the doors with a stretcher. It's covered with a white sheet. Whoever is under it is so tiny they might not exist at all.

I guess she doesn't exist, I think. Not anymore. Not the important parts of her. It's really sad. It is.

The stretcher jostles and something drops out of the sheet then catches on a long chain, tangled in a lock of long blond hair that looks dull and lifeless and dirty.

The bauble dangles there, swinging below the girl's shoulder, against the chrome of the rolling stretcher stand.

It is blue, glass. Completely unique. Only a single one like it in the whole world.

A Rue Michelle.

Amber's Rue Michelle.

Part of me cracks in half, then, the part of me that was Amber. It splits in two. I didn't even know she was still in me until the moment that section of my heart divided.

The part of me that hated Amber, hated what she did to Blake, hated what she did to me, it just goes away.

Disintegrates like ashes in a rainstorm. All that's left is an emptiness, a giant black cavern to fill with my tears.

She was my friend. She was almost my sister.

The part that's left, the part that glows when it sees her face, lights up just like she lights up everyone else, that part throbs and burns. Swollen and ready to burst, so much pressure I can barely take it.

Then it does burst.

"Amber," I say, soft at first, tears darting down my cheeks. Then, "Amber, Amber, Amber!"

Everyone in the crowd turns to look.

The tears are hot and fast now, so tight they're choking me so all I can do is scream.

"Amber! Amber! Amber!"

Then there's a hand on my shoulder. I look up into the kind eyes of a police officer.

52

THERE'S A BLANKET AROUND MY shoulders, a coffee cup in my hand, but I'm still shivering.

The officer brought me inside the building, past the crime scene tape like a bouncer at the worst possible dance club. Now we're sitting across from each other in one of the smaller classrooms that look more like a conference room because it only has one large table surrounded by lots of black rolling chairs. Me with my coffee, him with his notepad.

"Can I ask how you knew what happened today, Greta?" he says.

"I didn't—I—I was going to class, and I saw all the commotion. Then I saw her necklace, and I knew it was her."

"And the two of you are roommates?"

"Yes," I say. "Sort of. She's moving into the Kappa house. Spending most of her time there."

"We might want to take a look at your room. Would that

be okay?"

"Sure. Of course. Whatever I can do to help."

"Maybe this afternoon?"

"No problem."

I scan the room. There are red numbers scrawled on a whiteboard—a complex equation that looks like it could be from a trigonometry class. Everything in me wants to solve it right now. Because the equation is solvable. But this isn't. Amber isn't coming back.

"Great. So you said Amber was splitting her time between the dorms and the Kappa house. Where was she supposed to be last night?"

"At the Kappa house. She hasn't slept in the dorms with me for a couple weeks. She'd already moved some of her stuff out. She was going to move the rest out this weekend."

"Did you talk to her at all last night?"

"No. Not really."

"What does that mean?"

"I saw yesterday morning after breakfast, but not after that. It was her turn to do the lab so I didn't have to be there."

Our conversation replays in my mind. We were fighting. We were saying awful, awful things to each other. And it was the last time I'll ever hear her voice! Why didn't I try to make up with her? She would have understood about everything, especially Blake. She never really cared about him. She would have been happy for me.

"Your turn?" the officer asks.

"She was supposed to be covering a lab for me. We've been switching off so we don't have to do all of them," I say. So we didn't have to do them together would be closer to the truth. Then I catch myself and look at him. "It's not cheating."

"No, of course not," he says. "Don't worry, I'm not going to tell your teachers. I'm just looking for some information here, okay?"

"Okay," I say.

"So you guys were lab partners?

"Yes," I say.

"And she was taking her turn doing the lab?"

"Yes," I say.

I stare at the whiteboard, at those numbers again. I try to sort them out in my head, arrange them into something that makes sense, but they just blur together. Maybe nothing can be solved.

"Do you know what time she was planning to be there?"

"No. The labs are open until ten, but she usually does hers in the afternoon."

"So it was unusual for her to be there so late?"

"I guess so, yeah. She likes to party. I mean—not like that. She wasn't a bad person or anything."

The officer reaches out and pats me on the arm. "Like I said, Greta, I'm just looking for information. You can be honest with me."

"Okay," I say. "I am."

"Good. You were saying it was unusual for Amber to do

the Biology labs at night?"

"Yeah. She must have had some sorority thing earlier or something."

"Do you know what that could have been?"

If only I did. If only things had gone differently. If only we had done that lab together, had still been friends. Maybe then she would still be alive. But we weren't.

"No. I'm not in the sorority with her," I say.

"Okay. Did she tell you she was planning to meet anyone?"

"No."

"No one? Not a boyfriend or anything?"

"No."

"Do you know if Amber was seeing anyone?"

Then my face lights up. Of course. That boy. That terrible, terrible boy.

"She was," I say. "A boy from some house with a Zeta in it, I don't know much else. I think his name was Cam or Cameron or something."

"Do you know his last name?"

"No," I say. "But I didn't like him. I didn't like him at all."

The first thing I do is call Blake.

"Darling, call me back as soon as you can. It's an emergency. It's Amb—" I stop myself from saying her name. This isn't something he should learn about over the phone. However bad it was for them over the past few days, it will still be so hard to hear. He has such a compassionate soul. I have to find a way to protect him from it.

I text him just the numbers "911" ten times.

But he doesn't answer. Or call.

I'll go to him. I'll find him. I'll be there to comfort him when the ax falls.

53

I GRAB HIS FAVORITE COFFEE to soften the blow, a triple shot Americano, and walk toward the SigUp house. It's only a couple blocks away, but it's a challenge to carry our drinks without sloshing. Specks of hot liquid flick onto my hands with each step, leaving little red marks.

I drink mine down a bit, then take a sip out of his. It burns. It's so hot I have to spit it out on the sidewalk right in front of the house. I smack my lips, trying to cool them and trying to get the taste out. After the sweetness of my chai, his coffee bites with a lurid bitterness I can't handle. Someone on the porch guffaws. I hadn't noticed anyone there when I walked up.

"Whaddya got there?" a voice asks, amused.

His tone makes me tremble, sends me back to spitballs in my hair in eighth grade. I stride forward, trying to be confident. *I belong here now*, I tell myself. *I belong.*

"I'm here to see Blake," I say.

"Blake Houston?" he asks.

I suddenly can't remember his last name. It sits on the tip of my tongue, just barely not there.

"Yes," I say.

"No visitors today, sorry."

"Can you just tell him Greta Bell is here? I'm his girlfriend."

The guy wanders out from the shadows. He's lanky, smoking a joint, shirtless in spite of the cold. He looks me up and down.

"What did you say?"

"I'm his girlfriend. Greta Bell."

"No, you're not, sweetheart." He looks angry all of a sudden. He flicks the roach at me, so directly toward me I have to jump to miss it. Then he turns away. "Why don't you run along."

No. I won't let him get away with this. I belong here.

I follow him up to the door.

"You're seriously trying to follow me inside?" he says.

"Just tell him I'm here and I'll be out of your hair, okay?"

He spits, actually spits, right next to me. "It's not a good day, okay?"

"He's gonna be really pissed when he finds out—"

"Look, sweetie, I know you're not his girlfriend. You don't even know his last name. And frankly, it's kind of fucked up you're pretending to be."

"Abbott," I remember. "His last name is Abbott. I'm sorry. It's been a really stressful day."

"You need to go."

"I have his number in my phone. Look," I pull it out of my pocket and shove it toward him, but he doesn't take it.

"Jesus. Don't you watch the news? Blake's girlfriend was killed last night."

"No. You don't understand."

"Her name was Amber Benedict, not Greta whatever, and she was murdered. So I don't know what kind of fucked up game you're trying to play here, but it's time for you to go."

He goes inside, slams the door in my face. I'm reeling. His girlfriend? They think Amber was his girlfriend?

"Hey!" I say, reaching for the doorknob, which is already locked. "Blake?! Are you in there?!" My nose is pressed against the glass door. Maybe he's inside and will hear me. I have to talk to him. "Blake?!"

I see a shadowy figure lope down the grand staircase. Light blooms through the window behind him, and all I can make out is his silhouette, highlighted by the dust motes floating in the air around him. Still, it's him. I'd know the shape of him anywhere.

I knock harder. "Blake! Blake!"

"Sorry man," porch guy says to him inside. "Bitch out there is crazy."

"Who is she?" some other guy asks.

The figure comes closer to the glass. It's Blake for sure. I hear his voice, but the words are wrong.

"Her roommate. Just get rid of her, okay?"

Her roommate. Did he really just say that?

"Blake?"

"Jesus Christ. Get her the fuck out of here. I can't handle this right now." He sinks into a couch in a room to the left of the door. He puts his head in his hands.

My heart sinks.

Low, low, low.

The bottom of the ocean. Buried under the muck.

Then I see Tucker's face. He comes right up to the glass. I'm still pressed up against it, and his features distort in the cut panes, but I can tell it's him from his mushy body.

"Get out of here or I'm calling the cops," he says.

"No," I say. "I'm not leaving until I talk to him."

Inside, I can see a flip switch inside Tucker. He's pissed. He jabs for the knob. I realize too late the direction the door swings.

It opens into me, hard. The cups in my hands crush against me.

Hot coffee spills down my front, all over. It burns and, soaked into my clothes, doesn't stop burning.

I pull at my T-shirt to relieve the pain of it, but I don't have enough hands to make it stop. There are tears on my cheeks now, not just from the pain, but the humiliation too, and the injustice of it, and can Blake really not want to see me?

The guy from before is standing behind Tucker now, just staring at me. Staring, staring, like maybe they pushed me too far, like maybe he's sorry. The pity in his eyes is what does it.

"Fuck you!" I scream, "Fuck you!" And I know my face is the color of children's wagons and blinking open signs and the hot, hot sun. I know spit is forming at the corners of my mouth and my fists are balled into bombs. I know all this, but I can't stop.

"Fuck you! Fuck you! Fuck you!" Every scream is louder, crazier than the last and I can hear it, but I can't stop.

And the guy is still staring and Blake won't come out and I know I am ridiculous, again, as always. And I want to hit the boy and hit Tucker and hit Blake until he says my name and never hers again. But I know he won't. He will never say my name again.

So I hurl the empty cups at Tucker and I run. Away, away, as far as I can. There is a path that runs along the creek and I take it.

How dare he do this? How dare he?

54

MY SHIVERING FOCUSES ME. I huddle behind an overgrown blackberry bush, six feet tall and bare, the last of its fruit withered to rot, its leaves windblown. Creek water thunders past, flowing down from an early snowfall on the hills above. The din of it drowns out everything but my rage.

How dare he.

It is not a question; it's a declaration. I know the answer. I am bowled over by the force of it.

I can see so clearly now every step—the wine and the wooing. Especially the wooing. His arms and his mouth and his body against mine. All a price, not a gift.

He thinks he is done now. The worst is over; step fuck-over-Greta is complete. But he does not know the force of me. He does not know the things I want. He does not know the things I've done to get them.

I rise. The wind presses at my cheeks. I know exactly what to do, but I don't know if I'll have time. I have to hurry.

Part Nine

My Johnny

55

I TAKE EVERY PRECAUTION. IF I get caught doing what I'm about to do, then I will go to jail and doing it will have been for nothing.

So I'm careful. I make a plan.

I set the digital recorder at the gas station to tomorrow's date. The recorder records everything I do in grainy images from cameras set into the ceiling and pointed at the register in the glass cashier booth. Then I spend the whole day there, wearing a blue summer dress that sets off my hair perfectly.

At exactly three o'clock, I go into the back room and switch the DVD's in the drive like I do every day. Like everyone who works here does. Then I set the dates back to normal.

The next day, I wear the same dress, the same shoes. I fix my hair the same way, in long swingy, curls down my back. I wear the same lipstick. But I don't go to work. I go to a coffee shop in town. It's somewhere I can be seen, somewhere I can prove my presence with a receipt. I leave right before my shift was supposed to start. Even my parents don't know I paid Gary to switch shifts with him.

I even punched Gary's timecard yesterday, then hid it. I wrote my name on my own timecard in pencil, just so I could erase it and put his name on it for today. With the way he drinks, he won't remember the exact dates. He lives his whole life in a fuzz of alcohol.

I change in the car—tucking my hair into a dark cap and putting on jeans and a loose T-shirt.

I go to the hospital.

I'm not supposed to be there, the police have said so and my parents have said so and so have his parents. But who will notice a pretty girl who says she's there to visit her grandmother if anyone asks?

I am pretty now. I've made myself pretty in the two months he's been in the hospital. I can tell I have. I can tell by the way the customers look at me in the gas station, the way the men look at me like they haven't had a meal in weeks and I am top sirloin.

But my pretty isn't for them. It's for him. It's always been for Johnny. I wish that today I could show him how pretty I've become. But it's more important not to be recognized.

Getting into the hospital is no trouble. They don't even look at me as I pass the main reception counter. No one asks questions if you act like you know where you're going.

What's trickier is finding him.

The place is big, it serves everyone in our county and the

three neighboring counties too. But I've looked up the terms, and there are signs everywhere. In the end, it's so easy it's almost like he's calling me directly to him.

I know he's not.

I do.

I'm not crazy. Don't say I am.

He definitely isn't calling me. If he had called me even once—if he had answered any of my letters or friended me on Facebook or asked me to prom instead of *that girl*—then none of this would be happening. I wouldn't be here, smelling the stale chemical stench of the yellowing halls. I wouldn't have made a plan.

The thing Johnny needs is a wake-up call. It's like his ears are clogged. Or maybe his heart.

I find his room and walk in.

He's all alone, sleeping softly, his head bandaged. Parts of it are shaved to the skin. His beautiful hair! I miss it. He doesn't look the same without it. He looks older, less innocent.

I lean in and kiss him.

I caress his face, his beautiful face.

Then I light the match and drop it onto his bed and go.

56

I GIVE JOHNNY A FEW weeks to let my message sink in. It's not okay for him to treat me this way, but I believe in my heart we can get past this. The police came, but there wasn't anything they could do when I showed them the video from the gas station and my time card. The footage from the hospital only shows fuzzy images of someone who could either be a boy or a girl. And the fire didn't even make the news, so I know it couldn't have hurt him that bad. It was only a warning.

I pick a bright blue Saturday, the kind of day that was made for chirping birds and skipping children. Gary is in the gas station with me today. We always have two people in the store on Saturdays because it gets so busy. Gary is in his seventies and a drinker. He has trouble working the cash register sometimes and can't really do stocking because of how hard carrying the boxes is on his back. He doesn't really need a job, just wants something to do and likes cars, which makes him an acceptable employee as far as my parents are concerned. They've never seen what an asset I am to them, but they'll understand soon. I tell Gary I need to run an errand and will be back soon.

Both are a lie. If this works, I'll never be back. There's a suitcase in my trunk, an empty bank account that was full yesterday, a letter back home on my desk, and plenty of gas in the tank. All I need is him. We can leave now, I'll tell Johnny. Leave now and never look back. It's what we need. He knows we do.

I drive the familiar route to his house, wondering where we'll go first. Mexico? California? Florida? Somewhere hot, I think. Somewhere to drive this awful winter out of our bones for good. We'll spend the summer there, loving each other and soaking up the sun. It will be easy enough to get jobs.

In the fall, we'll go to college together. We might even be married by then and be able to find a little apartment together instead of getting stuck in the dorms with strangers. I can just imagine our little place, warm and cozy. We'll study together and cook together, all the little things we've been prevented from doing all this time. There might even be a baby one day. A little Johnny running around. Not too soon, of course. We have to think of his career first.

Oh, I can't wait to see his face again. I ache for it, have ached for this moment for what feels like years. The moment when we'll finally be together forever. If I could only see one thing forever, it would be his face.

Adrenaline pumps through my veins as I turn onto his

street. He's so close now; it's only moments before I can touch him, kiss him, tell him I'm sorry and everything will be okay from now on. As long as we're together, everything will be okay.

I park in front and see a man's back as it disappears around the corner of the house. Something's not right about him. I duck down low so he won't see me and feel a little tightness in my chest.

I can't put my finger on it right away, then it finally dawns on me. The man's hair is white, and he's shorter than either Johnny or Johnny's dad. He doesn't belong there. Is he trying to hurt them?

I get out of the car and race behind the house. No one will hurt my Johnny. Not if I can help it.

The man is setting something against the side of the house but turns to face me when he hears my footsteps.

"Who are you and what are you doing here?" I ask. I twist my face into anger. He can't scare me.

"This is my house," he says with a wry grin. "Who are you?"

"No, it's not. The Markhams live here. I know them. And I don't know you."

"Calm down, kid. There's nothin' to get upset about." There's fear in his eyes, I can feel it. "I bought this house last week. Moving in today."

"That's a lie," I say.

"See for yourself," he says, pointing to the thing he'd been carrying. The thing he'd propped up against the side of the house. It's a real estate sign. A smaller sign, screwed on top says: SOLD.

"No," I say. "No. That can't be right. He would have told me if they were moving."

"I don't know what to tell you, kid."

I race around to the front of the house, some other vision pulling at my memory. Then I see it. There are no curtains hanging in the windows. What once was framed in bright green and white stripes is empty and lifeless. I peer inside one of the windows. Everything's gone. The place is totally empty.

I hear the man's footsteps behind me and turn to meet him.

"Where did they go?" I say.

"Outta state somewhere. They didn't say. Seemed to be in a hurry about it, though. Something about their kids. I got the place for a song."

I collapse onto the grass. This can't be happening. How could his parents do this to me? How could Johnny let them? The tears are running down my cheeks before I know it.

"Look, kid, I'm real sorry you're upset about your friends. Is there somebody I could call for you?"

Why won't this asshole leave me alone? First he steals my Johnny's house and now he's trying to intrude on our personal business?

"Go away," I shout. "Just leave me alone!"

He shuffles his feet for a minute, then says, "Once again,

I'm sorry for your troubles. But my movers are gonna be here soon so I'm gonna have to ask you to run along."

"I'm not going anywhere until you tell me where he went."

"Look, I don't know what happened to your friends but it's time for you to—"

"He's not my friend! He's my soul mate."

"I don't care what he is. You need to get off my property. Now."

"I can't go anywhere. I have to wait for him here until he comes back. He will come back for me. I know he will."

"You want me to call the police?"

No police. I can't handle all those questions again. All that prodding. And their stupidity! They'd never understand how evil Johnny's parents are. How much they hate him for finding happiness.

I grab a rock, get up, and hurl it at the man.

"Hey now!" he screams.

He dodges the rock and I run back to my car.

"Get the hell away from here and don't you come back!" he shouts at my back.

I get in the car and drive home. It is the most defeated I've ever felt in my life. I hate Johnny's parents and Johnny's little sister and my parents too. For a little while, I even hate Johnny. But only for a little while.

One day, we will find each other. One day, we'll be together. I just know it.

Part Ten

My Blake

57

I RACE TO THE DORM, go in through the back door as someone else is coming out. The room is down the hall, on the right. We all hate this hallway. By Tuesday, the stench of weekend parties—the stale pizza boxes and beer bottle fumes and old towels dried crack-hard with vomit—seeps through the well-sealed joints and into the corridor. There isn't an air freshener strong enough to combat it.

But I want to smell it. I need to. The familiar scent stings my nose as I get closer. I hope what I'm inhaling isn't a trick of hope. If they've come already, it's over.

I open the door and am in luck. The bin bulges with trash. But how will I ever find it?

There is an arm to shove the loads forward so they don't pile too high. I have no idea how often it runs. Once a day? Twice? Whether my bag is on the top or bottom depends entirely on the schedule. I have no time to find out and no desire to call attention to this task. It is pointless anyway, I decide, because to get to the bottom I'll have to go through the top. I think about space, divide the bin by seven days. My bag is most likely to be near the back, the sixth out of seven sections.

I dive in—a feral creature—tearing through trash before the evidence of my innocence is taken away forever. I shove aside the grocery bags, handles tied together but still overflowing with tissues and magazines and food waste. I shove aside boxes for televisions and hair dryers and care packages from Mom. I shove aside department store bags emptied of their purchases and takeout containers that reek with rotting food. Some sort of Chinese noodles spill down my front, bursting through the soaked and weakened bottom of a paper box.

What's left are the trash bags. But all of them look the same: white with yellow ties, just like mine. I concentrate on what's inside my bag, keep my eyes open for the familiar shapes, the red bulges showing through the stretch of the plastic. I grab bag after bag after bag, but I don't see it.

There is a grating sound and a rumble and a beep-beep-beep. Light enters the room, first from the floor, then an entire wall of it so bright it burns my eyes and my vision blotches to blurred dots as the loading dock door cranks open.

They're here.

I should go, but I'm so close. Maybe another foot separates me from feeling the grease-caked metal below my feet. I claw and throw, less careful now. I have to find it. It's my last chance.

There's a hard clunk, and I look up to see the truck. It's latching forklift-type claws to the top of the bin. A jostle throws me against the wall, and trash tumbles into the valley I've created, burying me chest-deep.

Then I see it. My bag—and I'm sure it's mine because the stretch of it reveals its contents—peeking out from the back corner.

I hoist myself up on the rim, tilting slowly now toward the truck's open mouth.

"Hey! Lady! Hey!" I hear a voice shouting at me from the passenger window. "Stop the lift, Larry! Stop it!"

It stops. There's a lurch and grind as it reverses toward the ground. The trash pile topples toward the back, about to cover my bag again. I can't lose it.

I dive for the bag, landing on something hard that jabs into my side. The trash starts to bury me again, this time my face too. But both my hands are on it.

I struggle through to the top, clutching it tight. My breath comes hard, and I look up to see blue eyes under wrinkled, heavy brows.

"What the heck are you doin' in there, lady?! You coulda' got yourself crushed!"

"Sorry. I'm sorry. I accidentally threw out the wrong bag."

I toss the bag out and throw myself over the wall. My side screams with the motion. I rush to the bag and peek inside to be sure. It's there. It's all there.

I look back and see the two trash men staring at me,

mouths open. I must be a sight. Coffee-soaked, tear-stained, trash-tousled.

"I'm sorry," I say again, bolting to the door with the bag.

"Jeez-Louise," I hear the not-Larry man say on my way out. "These friggin' kids these days."

I race to my room. Perhaps it was foolish not to go here first, I think. Perhaps the police have been here and have already found what I'm sure *I* will find if they haven't.

I open the door and it is empty, my things untouched, unruffled, no tape on the door to secure it for evidence.

I close the door behind me. My breath catches in my throat as I glance at the mirror. I don't recognize myself I'm so dirty. There are leaves in my hair, and dirt from the ground, a garbage-soaked T-shirt, and rot smears on my skin. But I don't have time to clean myself now. They will be here soon, I'm sure of it.

I start to look. It will not be with her things. It will be with mine.

I rifle through my coat pockets, empty my laundry basket. The room is small, but there are thousands of hiding places, it seems. I check my desk drawers, under my bed, on the top of the wardrobe and underneath it. At some point my hands fasten on those glasses—the ones from the very first night we met—and I put them on to make me feel stronger.

I have to be careful as I go. If they come in, I cannot risk the place looking like a mess.

I pull out the drawers, feel the walls inside the desk. I turn the chair over. I pull the mattress away from the wall.

And there it is. Taped to my box spring inside a Ziploc bag is the letter opener, the one from Amber's desk set. There's blood on it.

I throw the bloody bag into my backpack.

I open the trash bag and take out the things I need, touching them as little as possible in the process. Red Solo cups, the residue of what he gave me still inside, his fingerprints surely there too. An empty bottle of wine. The used condom.

I lay the items on my bed and take a picture of them with my phone. One snap, so many consequences. But not for me.

Then I put them into a fresh trash bag and place it in my backpack with the letter opener and the rest of the desk set—which might raise suspicion with just the knife missing. I bring his glasses too.

I change into a fresh set of clothes and put the old ones in a different trash bag I'll toss on my way out. There are tender red patches from the coffee all down my chest, bright flares that mar my otherwise creamy skin. I hate them.

I tug my hair into a ponytail and throw on sunglasses to hide my dirty face and go. There isn't time for more.

58

I KNOCK ON HER DOOR, a big old brick and cedar craftsman—too big for just her, but she can afford it. My backpack sits on my shoulder. It is nearly one in the afternoon. Aunt Peggy will still be at work; the knock is just to verify she's not home. I dig the extra key out of my pocket and go inside.

The card I'm looking for is in the kitchen junk drawer. I take it and leave.

I open the door to WellSpring—Aunt Peggy's fancy gym/spa—and immediately the scent of lavender hits me. I use the card from her house to get inside, past a receptionist who barely glances up from her magazine to say, "Welcome, Ms. Danforth. Have a great workout." She must be reading it from the computer screen.

But I'm not looking for a yoga class or a steam room today. I'm looking for a locker.

I enter the locker room. There's no one here right now;

I'm lucky. The lockers are solid wood, bamboo I think. I choose the first one, closest to the door. I put my backpack inside and secure it with a lock. This isn't the kind of place that cuts off the locks. They have more lockers than members. I won't be able to leave it here forever, but this should buy me a few days.

I decide I have time now. Now that I have what I need. Now that I'm away from there.

I take off my clothes. I enter a shower stall and pull the curtain and start the water. I let it run until the water goes clear under my feet and I can think straight again. I finger the burns on my skin, let the pain of it prick me awake.

This is happening. This is really happening.

I have to focus. I get out of the shower, dress again, do my best to look normal. His glasses are on my face now. The backpack stays behind.

I make one more stop—to the drug store—before going home. I use the back door again, waiting for another student to leave so I don't have to use my keycard to get back inside. When I arrive at my room, the police are still not here. *This will work*, I think. *This will work.*

I text the picture I took earlier to Blake. I have to be careful—word it just right—in case they are watching.

Missing Amber so much. Can't believe any of this. Been cleaning to keep from crying and found your present.

Come see me? Not doing great.

Kisses.

There's a knock on my door as soon as I press send. It's

the police.

59

WE'RE IN ONE OF THOSE rooms you see on TV—one with the glass mirror that's not a mirror at all. I wonder who's behind it, watching me. I wonder who else was here before me. They must be talking to all her friends, but maybe especially me.

"The thing is, Greta, we've talked to a lot of people. And most of them had stories to tell us about you." The detective's name is Bob Cole, but he reminds me of Tom Selleck. He has that mustache only guys pushing sixty and hipsters under thirty seem to favor. He's the former.

"What kind of stories?" I say.

"Stories about you having a particular interest in Amber's boyfriend, Blake. Stories about you maybe not taking it so well that he picked her over you."

"He changed his mind," I say. "In fact, he was with me last night. In my room."

"I doubt it," he says. "Woulda' been awful tricky to pull that off."

I wrinkle my brow, confused. "Of course he was with me. Why would I lie?"

"Several people can confirm Blake was at a party which took place last night at the, ah …" he picks up a notepad, "Sigma Phi Upsilon house on Grant Street. Apparently, he's a member of the fraternity."

I try not to let my face register my surprise. This I didn't expect. He was more careful than I thought.

"We call it SigUp," I say.

"I have over twenty independent witnesses that claim to have seen him. Reports begin at a quarter to eight, when he helped with setup. The last report clocks in at just after five in the morning when he was seen exiting his room with a girl named Jessica."

"Jessica James?" I ask. My Rho Chi? Gorgeous, fawn-colored Jessica James? I have to fight to keep the fire from bursting through my throat like a dragon.

"That's correct."

"She's lying. She's been trying to get with Blake all year." But Blake has a resolution now, one I intend to help him keep.

"It wasn't Miss James who provided the information. It was her friend, Whitney Cummings, and the young man whose room Whitney spent the night in, Ivan Blane. Both Whitney and Ivan witnessed Jessica and Blake exiting the room together the following morning. This matches the testimony we received from Blake himself."

"Maybe he misspoke. Blake kicked her out of his room

this morning when he got home. She passed out there after the party," I say. It sounds true, doesn't it? "He was with me last night."

Detective Bob pulls out a laptop. The screen flashes on, and there he is. Blake, my Blake, dressed in white boxer briefs and a white bow tie. A hot pink smiley face winks on his stomach under black lights. It's a highlighter party.

Detective Bob presses a button and another photo appears. This time Blake does a keg stand with his frat buddies.

In another, Blake and Jessica grind against each other. There's a neon orange kiss on his cheek, the same color as her garish lips. His hand is on her waist, his thumb hooked in the waistband of her impossibly tiny skirt.

Then another of them together, this one even worse than the last. There's a crowd around him screaming. Jessica is rolling her eyes but really loving the whole thing. Blake's right hand is cupping her left breast. With his left hand, he's using a highlighter to draw an outline of his grip onto her bright white T-shirt.

Detective Bob keeps clicking. The photos go on and on.

"Not the most dedicated boyfriend, if you ask me," he says.

"Blake and I don't get caught up in labels," I say. "I don't care who he's with, sexually. I've had other men too. But I know who he really loves."

He clicks the slideshow one last time and there she is. Amber lies on the floor of the science lab, eyes frozen forever, tiny slits in her skin like she's been attacked by a flock of birds.

"Maybe it's time to stop with the lies," he says.

"Excuse me?" I try to act surprised and offended, but I knew where this was heading.

Blake has been a bad boy. A very, very bad boy.

60

I LOOK UP FROM THE computer screen, right at Detective Cole, forcing him to believe me. But I can't forget what I've seen. All those pictures stab my heart to pieces. I want to delete them from existence. But it wouldn't matter, they've already happened. And things are different now, after seeing them.

I look into the mirror that's not a mirror. The glasses make me strong, Clark-Kent me into being Superman. I know what I want too, and what I need. And I know how to get it. *Just like you Blake, just like you.*

"Okay, you're right. I haven't been totally honest with you. And neither has Blake, apparently."

The tears that come to my eyes aren't fake.

"All right," Detective Cole says. "I'm listening."

"It's true I wasn't happy they got together. I love Blake. I really do. I've loved him since the first time I saw him. So much it hurts sometimes."

The detective sets his lips into a hard line.

"But I would never hurt Amber. I would never do that."

"Where were you last night, Miss Bell?"

"I was with him. That part wasn't a lie."

He leans back in his chair and crosses his arms.

"But we weren't in my room. We were in his."

"Is that so?"

"He probably didn't want to tell you. Because you're obviously just going to think he did it, right? I mean, they got into a big fight just a couple days ago. Over me, really. You probably talked to him first, didn't you? And if he said he was with me, that would look even worse."

"Miss Bell, if you were at that party, then why haven't I heard about it from anyone else?"

"Because I wasn't at the party. I was just in his room. We weren't telling anyone about our relationship because it made Amber so upset before. It was just, like, a lot of drama we didn't want, you know? So we kept it a secret. I guess we thought she'd cool off after a few days, maybe find someone else. I was just doing homework up there until he could get away."

"And Jessica James?" This is the hardest part, but I have to say it. "I guess … we're not a traditional couple, Blake and I. We like things, just … different. I like to watch. I like to watch him with other women."

Detective Cole raises his eyebrows.

"I know it's unusual. But Blake indulges me. I think he likes it too, really. What man wouldn't?"

"So you're saying you were in the room, but Jessica

wasn't aware of it?"

"I really don't know. She seemed pretty drunk."

"Where were you in the room?"

My heart beats extra fast. I've never actually been inside Blake's room, just glimpsed it that time Amber was with him. I strain to remember the details. What did I see? A bed. Amber in his bed, sheets covering her body. A lamp. A dresser, a tall one.

"I was standing behind his dresser."

"And how was it that Miss James spent the entire night in the room without realizing you were there?"

"She passed out pretty fast afterward, and I left before she woke up. I had to get changed for class."

The door slams open.

It's Blake.

His face is white. He's out of breath. His eyes lock on mine.

"I told them everything," I say, my face going hard. I want to make him stew.

He sets his jaw, takes in a breath to make himself taller. I can see his mind working—that brilliant mind—trying to come up with a way out of this.

"They know I was in your room last night, watching you with Jessica. I'm sorry. I had to tell them," I say.

A chubby police officer jogs up behind him. "Sorry about that sir, he just barged in."

"I know it looks bad, but we both really loved Amber—cared about her I mean," I say. I did love her, I realize.

Blake did too. He must have, to hurt her that way. I know what it's like.

"I'm sorry about what I told you before, Officer," Blake says. "I got scared and I panicked. I'd like to update my statement. My lawyer will be here shortly to get everything straightened out."

Detective Cole looks from one of us to the other with a stern, suspicious expression on his face.

"You'll excuse me if I tell you I'm having a very hard time believing that."

He may not believe us, but it takes more than disbelief to convict someone. It takes bloody letter openers or red solo cups laced with Rohypnol, and he doesn't have them.

Blake turns to me, "If Detective Cole refuses to listen to the truth, it might be best if we stopped talking without a lawyer present."

They separate us, try to question me again, but I'm a good listener. I don't say a word. Then Blake's lawyer arrives and argues with the detectives for a long time. Eventually, they let us both leave. What else can they do?

"This isn't over," Detective Cole says. "We will need to speak to you both again. I expect you to stay close. Both of you."

"We're happy to cooperate, officer," Blake says. "I apologize for all the confusion."

"Hold on now," the lawyer says to Blake. "Unless you have an arrest warrant, my clients are free to do as they wish."

The lawyer and Detective Cole start fighting again, but I've heard all I need to hear.

I go to Blake, take his hand in mine.

"Ready to go?" I ask.

He looks up at me warily, not sure if this is a trick.

"Come on. It's been a long day," I say.

61

BACK AT MY DORM, HE vibrates with fear. He's afraid of me, I realize. I'm surprising him again.

"Where is it?" he asks.

"Safe," I say.

"I'll pay you. Whatever you want. I have money."

"Hush," I say. He stops.

I unwrap a tiny box and hand him the small tube inside. It's burn cream. It will help.

I take off my shirt.

He is gentle with my body this time. He smooths the salve into the burns with the utmost care.

"Is that what you want?" he asks.

"Darling," I say.

"What?"

"Call me darling."

"Is that what you want, darling?" he asks.

"Yes," I say.

"So what now?" he asks. "What do you want?"

"Now?" I ask. "Now we love each other. Forever and ever."

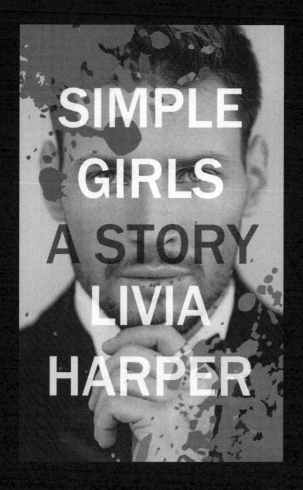

CAN'T WAIT FOR MORE? HERE'S a sneak peak at what Greta and Blake are up to next…

PARTY DRESS

Livia Harper

1

I WISH AMBER WERE HERE.

She always knew so much about clothes, which ones would look good on me, and which ones weren't worth the hanger they were hung on. She would have walked right into this department store and known just what to get. She would have picked the perfect outfit to wear to Blake's fall formal.

But Amber isn't here to help. And I don't know what to wear.

It's been two weeks since she died, since Blake did what he did so that we could be together. Eight days ago they shipped her body back to South Carolina for the funeral. Blake didn't think it was a good idea for us to go, but we watched it on TV. Everyone watched it on TV—the perfect southern belle laid to rest before her time, her parents holding each other as they cried over her casket, her sorority sisters clutching their pearls. And seven hundred miles north, a college campus clamoring for answers.

But I'm the only one with answers, and I'm not telling.

I paw through racks of dresses, searching for the perfect one. But I don't know what it looks like. Everything in the store, in every store up until now, just feel off.

"How about this one?" Blake sighs, holding up a short cocktail dress with sapphire sequins. I want to laugh, the sight is so sweet. He's trying to be patient, I can tell, but we've been at this all morning, and even the most patient man has his limits. His face is stony, his jaw set. There's a crease between his brows that grows deeper by the minute.

I shake my head and smile. "No. It has to be perfect," I say.

"At least try something on," he says. "We don't have all day. The bus leaves at four."

"Relax, baby," I say, leaning in to kiss him. "Don't you want me to look perfect for you?"

"It's not brain surgery, Greta. It's a dress. Just pick something for Christ's sake."

His face has gone red as cherries, the blue dress crumpled in his fist.

"I will," I say. "I'll know it when I see it." But I'm not sure if that's true.

I wander farther down the aisle, looking to see if anything will catch my attention. There are miles of lace and satin and tulle and chiffon. A year ago, I would have been happy with any of them, ecstatic to even be going to an event like this, but now I have higher standards. Tonight is the first time we'll be in public, truly in public, as a couple. The dress has to shine. It has to show everyone why Blake chose me. And nothing, nothing at all, seems right.

"You don't have to go if you don't want to, you know. These things can be really boring. I mean, I have to because I'm chapter president, but there's no reason you have to subject yourself to that."

"Don't be silly," I say. "Of course I'm coming. I couldn't make you go to something like this by yourself. People will expect me to be there."

"Have it your way," he says.

Then, nestled between two black frocks on the discount rack, I spot something. It is frosty blue tulle and sparkles with glittery silver sprinkled on the skirt like sugar. I pull it out to look closer and my heart races. The only thing missing is the bow.

It's a sign. It must be a sign.

"This one," I say to Blake, my eyes shining. "This is the one."

"Finally," he says.

I bring the dress to the checkout desk.

"Can I help you?" the saleswoman says.

"Yes. Do you have a seamstress on staff that could make a slight alteration? I need it today."

The saleswoman calls in the seamstress and they work on my dress while I go to the salon to have my hair done. Once you find the dress, the rest is so much easier: shoes, necklace, earrings, tiara, gloves. Everything else came together in an instant. Blake, being the generous boyfriend he is, paid for everything of course.

I have the beautician curl and pile my hair into a high updo, the tiara nestled in a twist of silky red curls at my crown. She glosses my lips and pinks my cheeks and shimmers my eyes. She paints my fingers and my toes and sends me out the door looking better than Amber was ever able to make me look.

I'm so excited as I head back toward the department store for my dress that I almost don't notice him. He comes right up beside me. How could he have known to find me here?

"Hi there, Greta." It's the detective, the one with the mustache. Jim Drummond.

I scowl at him, "What do you want?"

"Just thought we could discuss a few things."

"I don't have to talk to you. I have a lawyer. I know my rights."

"What do you have to be worried about? You had nothing to do with Amber's death, right?"

"Of course not. I was with Blake the whole night."

"Well, not the whole night, right?"

"He wasn't at the party for very long. You know that."

"I'm not so sure, Greta. I'm really not."

"Well, I'm sure."

"Just seems curious, don't you think? You thought you spent the whole night with him, but we have pictures—lots of pictures—of him at that party."

"Like I said, he had to make an appearance. He was downstairs until people got drunk enough not to notice anymore. You probably couldn't get into a fraternity when you were in college, so you can't know what those parties are like, but getting that drunk doesn't exactly take very long. Plus, he had to get Jessica. That took a little time."

"Okay, so that first time we talked? Why were you so sure he'd been with you all night?"

"You mean while you were accusing me of murdering my best friend? Is that the time you're talking about?"

"What made you think that he'd been with you all night, Greta? Did you pass out? Did he give you something? Is that why you thought you'd been together the whole time?"

"Are you accusing my boyfriend of—? This is ridiculous."

"Here's the thing, Greta. We got in touch with a girl, doesn't go to this school anymore. She says Blake put something in one of her drinks one night. She woke up the next morning in his room, didn't remember how she got there."

"Lots of girls want to be with Blake. And lots of girls are upset when they don't stay together forever."

"But he's with you now, right?"

"That's right."

"That was mighty fast."

"True love has no time for doubts."

"I guess if I were you, I'd be a little concerned about being with a guy like that. Seems like there's a real good reason to have some doubts."

"I don't have to listen to this." I turn back to the sidewalk and pick up my pace, but his legs are longer than mine—thin and fast as a spider's. He doesn't have to even try to keep up.

"Just one more question, Greta."

"I told you, I'm done with your questions."

"Why is it that no one on campus seems to think you two were dating until after Amber died?"

"We kept it quiet for the first week. Amber was my roommate. She had just been dating Blake. We didn't want to upset her."

"Didn't want to upset her or didn't want it to look like you'd been going together behind her back?"

"So are you saying that we *weren't* dating or are you saying that we planned to kill Amber together? Which is it?"

"Woah, now. Settle down. I didn't say anything like that. But I sure am curious why you jumped to that conclusion."

"I didn't—I wasn't—"

"Is there anything you need to tell me, Greta?"

"No."

"People are talking, you know. A lot of people. They think there's something off about the two of you. They think it's real strange how a girl like you and a guy like him end up together."

"What's that supposed to mean?"

"It's just, well, you were never really very popular, were you? You don't fit in with Blake's crowd."

"Shut up," I say. "I don't have to talk to you. I want my lawyer."

"Hey, there's no need for—"

"I said I want my lawyer. If you want to keep talking to me, then I want my lawyer."

"Okay, alright. Have it your way." He hands me his business card. "But here's my number if you want to talk."

I rip it up into tiny pieces and throw it at his feet.

"I don't."

2

IT TAKES ME A MOMENT to catch my breath.

You don't fit in.

You don't fit in.

You don't fit in.

What if Detective Drummond was right? What if I don't fit in with Blake's crowd? Tonight is the first time we'll really be spending time with his friends. What if they don't like me? I couldn't stand it.

Just in time, I catch a glimpse of my reflection in a shop window. I almost don't recognize myself. I look stunning. Regal. Like a princess. And Blake is my prince.

I am a princess.

I am a princess.

I am a princess.

I shouldn't have spoken to the detective. Blake warned me not to. His lawyer warned me not to. I should have known they would put lies into my mind. Stupid, useless lies.

I just have to put them out of my head.

I am a princess.

I am a princess.

I am a princess.

A princess doesn't listen to lies.

I walk the remaining three blocks to the store with my head held high.

When I put on the dress, everything is perfect. The gown is tea-length with a trim waistline and a full skirt, like a movie star in the 1950's would wear. Where the waistline was once bare and boring, I've had them add a white satin sash, tied in the back with a large bow whose ribbons trail to the hemline.

I fasten the diamonds at my neck and slide on the white satin opera gloves.

I do look like a princess. A real, true princess.

I walk out of the dressing room to Blake like I'm walking on clouds. He's in a slim modern suit that makes him look like a runway model.

When he sees me, his eyes grow wide. His jaw hits the floor. Maybe he didn't know I could look so beautiful.

"How do I look?" I ask, my grin as wide as the grand canyon.

It takes him a moment to say anything. Then he pulls himself together and says, "Wow. That's…um…that's quite a dress."

"I told you it would be worth it. Didn't I tell you it would be worth it?"

"You did," he says.

I take his lapels in my hands and tug myself up until my lips meet his. He's so tall it's like climbing the rope in gym class to reach his mouth.

"Oh, my darling. I want to be so perfect for you. Tell me how perfect I am for you?"

"You're perfect," he says.

"Tell me I'm your princess," I say.

"You're my princess."

When we walk up to the buses that will drive us into New York City, there is a crowd of other students waiting, duffel bags strewn at their feet. SigUp has chartered a yacht to sail around the New York Harbor for the dance, then we're all spending the night at a hotel in the city called Hotel De La Fontaine.

The crowd turns to gape. I can see us through their eyes: Him dashing, tall and strong. His sunglasses mirroring the clear blue November sky, his crisp black suit cutting a dark silhouette against it the way the cold air cuts through the otherwise sunny day. And me on his arm, so ethereal and regal I must look like I was born of the blue over his head. We make a stunning picture together.

As I glance through the crowd, I can see that I am, by far, the best-dressed girl here. No one else has even made an effort compared to me. Their dresses are short, barely dressy enough to even be considered formal. Their hair and makeup look no different than any other night out at a random party. This is what they wear to a formal gala? Don't they care at all about the young men they're supposed to be accompanying? Don't they realize what they wear reflects directly on SigUp? SigUp isn't just some lower-rung fraternity. It's a storied brotherhood with a reputation to uphold. There are standards for these boys, high ones. And the women here are a total disappointment. I may have to get Blake to let me have a chat with them.

I squeeze his arm, happy for him that he's not with a lesser woman. I'm proud I'm the one on his arm, and proud I've taken on the mantle of living up to the expectations being with a man like Blake brings.

There's a snort from somewhere, a girl in slut-red flapper fringe. The two other girls next to her—in sequined cocktail dresses so short they barely cover their nasties—roll their eyes and cross their arms over their chests. Jealousy is so unattractive.

Tucker, Blake's frat brother and a former friend of Amber's, ambles through the crowd toward us, his dirty-looking mop of hair rippling in the breeze, a flask in his hand. The over-confident stride on his stumpy, baby-faced body reminds me of everything I hate about him. But he lost our little battle and I won. I try to remember not to be a sore winner. Besides, now that I'm with Blake, it all seems so petty. So small.

"Well if it isn't the prom king and queen in the flesh," he says, his voice booming through the air.

More snorts from the crowd. Are they laughing? At what?

I don't get the joke. They're probably just ribbing Blake, giving him a hard time because he's so in love. But when I glance at Blake, his jaw is set firmly and his eyes are steel.

"You sure this is a good idea, man?" Tucker asks, glaring in my direction.

Blake inhales a deep breath through his nose and plants his chin high. "Don't we call you barf boy or something? Remember who you're speaking to, fuckface."

"Sorry, man. Just trying to help a brother out."

"Help? Really? Let me tell you something, *brother*. I'm not gonna go around acting like a fucking loser just because the police asked me some questions. I don't give a fuck what little shits like you think. I have nothing to be ashamed of."

Tucker glances at me, then back at Blake. "Okay. Whatever you say."

Only his eyes aren't saying, "Whatever you say." They're saying, "Fuck you."

ABOUT THE AUTHOR

When she's not hanging out with her ginger husband and two stinky basset hounds, Livia Harper writes modern thrillers and mysteries. She's a film lover and award-winning screenwriter with a degree in Writing & Directing from Colorado Film School. She's also a graduate of UCLA's Professional Program in Screenwriting. For a long time, she made her living as a photographer, but today she's happy to call herself a writer. She's overjoyed to be sharing her books with you, and plans on many more to come.

Never miss a new release from Livia!

Sign up now at

www.LIVIAHARPER.com

for updates and freebies only available to subscribers.

ALSO AVAILABLE FROM LIVIA HARPER...

SLAIN

Pastor's daughter Emma Grant can almost taste freedom. Soon she'll graduate high school and give up prayer rallies and purity balls forthe halls of NYU and a new life. But when her friend is murdered, Emma becomes the prime suspect. And if she doesn't find the killer, she may be the next victim.

More in the GRETA BELL series

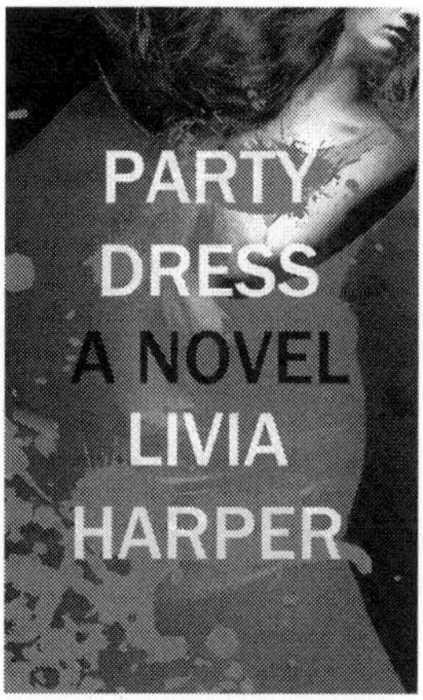

PARTY DRESS (book 2)
Greta has her man, but paradise isn't all she dreamed of. Everyone still thinks she killed Amber. Especially the police. And Blake is having a hard time adjusting to life as a couple. Will she end up alone—or worse—after fighting so hard for love?

DIAMOND RING (book 3)
Greta can't take her eyes off the sparkling ring on her finger. She's blissfully happy until her future inlaws forbid their son from marrying her. Greta doesn't need his family. Or their money. But as the big day approaches, he's having cold feet too. Very cold.

11512351R00210

Made in the USA
Monee, IL
12 September 2019